THE
STARGAZING
HOTEL

When you think you know
someone…

L.A. DONAHOE

COVER IMAGES:
Concierge Bell by Fer Gregory, www.shutterstock.com (Image ID: 1697799046)
Hotel Sign by theendup, www.shutterstock.com (Image ID: 662843557)

Cover and layout design by Jenny Engwer, *First Choice Books*
Author photo by L.A. Donahoe

Issued in print and electronic formats.

ISBN: 978-0-2285-0409-2 (paperback)
ISBN: 978-0-2285-0410-8 (html)

Printed in Canada ♻ on recycled paper
 FIRST CHOICE BOOKS

firstchoicebooks.ca
Victoria, BC

10 9 8 7 6 5 4 3 2 1

With love to my son who always cheers me on.

JOSH DONAHOE

∽)C⌣

Special thanks to:

W. BASTIAN, L. CLARKE, S. DONAHOE, A. REID,
J. RICH, G. WARFORD, L.M. WATSON

THE
STARGAZING
HOTEL

ONE

"HI TONY, I JUST BOARDED the train again after our layover."

"Does Francine know where, or why, you're going?"

"No, and whatever you do, don't say a word. I don't want them knowing that I'm actually away to get mother's estate wrapped up at long last. I need to get this done without any further resistance from them. So, as far as they're concerned, I'm away on vacation."

"Sophie, I just can't see that response working with Francine or Tyler. You know how your sister and brother-in-law can be."

"Tony, you've been my assistant for a very long time, you've dealt with far more difficult people than Francine and Tyler. Why are you so concerned about them?"

"Why? Because we both know that they are absolutely relentless. Don't you remember the time when they were on the board of directors and they pushed to have a motion passed to the point where they were calling board members at their homes day and night for weeks? I had angry board members calling me constantly telling me to get them off their backs. You know what they can be like."

"I do know, yes, which is why I have you to deal with them. Besides, they're no longer on the board of directors. In fact, they are no longer employees of Callaghan Hotels. They're silent partners. That's it. So it should be pretty easy to avoid them now. Be creative."

Sophie could hear Tony sighing over the phone and grinned.

"Okay, but you do realize that you are putting me in a position to ask you for another pay increase."

"I do realize that, yes."

"And you will have to give it to me because I deserve it."

"I realize that as well, yes."

"Okay then, fine. I'll let you know how much I want and, in the meantime, I will be 'creative' as you so succinctly put it."

"Good luck with that, Tony."

"Gee, thanks."

Sophie chuckled as she hung up. His sarcasm was evident and Sophie smiled thinking about Tony venting his frustrations. She would be lost without him and they both knew it so, yes, he would be getting his pay increase because he was worth every penny.

Looking up, she watched as a very distinguished older gentleman sat down across from her.

"Where are you off to, young lady?"

"Granite Hill, and you?"

"Same."

Sophie watched as he removed his gloves one finger at a time then carefully folded them, placing them in his overcoat pocket. It was an expensive overcoat she could tell, cashmere to be exact. Her father had owned one very similar. Unbuttoning his coat he removed it and carefully placed it over the seat beside him, followed by the silk scarf from around his neck.

He was a well-groomed gentleman, clean shaven, with a full head of salt and pepper hair, carefully trimmed and combed back with a part to one side.

"And what prompted you to travel by train?"

"Pardon me?" Sophie had difficulty hearing. The train whistle echoed the moment the trolley cart wheeled past them in the aisle. Glasses on the cart clinked together from the jerking of the train as it pulled out of the station, while the cans of pop and juice bounced around in the tray of ice they had been stuffed into.

"I was just curious why you opted to travel by train?"

Sophie didn't feel the man was prying, just making conversation and she was anxious to speak to anyone.

Other than Tony, my trip so far has been pretty much conversationless. Was that even a word? Regardless, the conversation is wholeheartedly welcome.

"It seemed to be the more relaxing mode of transportation. Besides, I especially love it this time of year, with all of the leaves on the trees changing colour. The autumn is such a beautiful time of year to see the countryside."

That was only partly true but Sophie didn't feel the need to get into the details with a stranger about her fear of flying. "It's quite a lovely way to travel although I'm not so sure about the food."

"Oh? Why is that?"

"Even in first class the food leaves a lot to be desired." She smiled.

"Ah yes, well, admittedly, the sandwiches are a bit soggy. I did give them a go with much regret." The man nodded. "Let me introduce myself. My name is Winston."

"Nice to meet you, Winston. My name is Sophie." Shaking his hand, Sophie leaned back in her seat and took a moment to look out her window and check the view, which at this very moment was the back walls of city buildings lined with many garbage dumpsters.

"Is that short for Sophia?"

"Yes, it is."

"That was my mother's name. Sophia Maria Lombardi."

"That's a beautiful name."

"She was a beautiful woman." Winston smiled with pride.

Checking his watch, Winston nodded. "It seems we will be right on time arriving into Granite Hill this afternoon. Admittedly, I won't be disappointed to get home and enjoy my own bed this evening."

"You live in Granite Hill?"

"That I do. And what brings you to my home town, Miss Sophie?"

Thinking it over, Sophie offered as little information as possible. "Family."

"You have family there? Wonderful. I'm sure they will be happy to see you and you will certainly love our city. There is plenty to see and do. You won't be disappointed."

"I've been there before. I worked there for a couple of years awhile back, actually."

"Where does your family live? Will you be staying with them?"

"No, I'll be staying at the C-Granite Hotel." Sophie smiled.

"Ah yes, that's a lovely hotel - top-notch, really. Quite modern, with approximately twelve hundred rooms to choose from. Nice location downtown - you can walk just about everywhere from the C-Granite. Great view of the mountains not to mention, it's quite popular with political delegations that return each year. You've made a good choice to stay there."

Sophie smiled. "So, you grew up in Granite Hill, I take it?"

CHAPTER ONE

"Oh yes, indeed. I've lived there my whole life. Couldn't imagine being anywhere else. My family has lived there since before I was born."

Sophie sat and listened while Winston went over his family history. It was interesting. She was enjoying her conversation with him. He was a sweet ole guy.

"My wife never did like me to fly…"

"Your wife didn't come on this trip with you?" Sophie was curious about the woman who was married to this rather extraordinary gentleman.

"No, my dear. My wife died several years ago."

Sophie saw the sadness envelop his eyes. They suddenly looked distant as he glanced out the window.

"I'm sorry. I shouldn't have asked…"

"Now, don't you worry about that at all. Actually, my wife often travelled with me. She loved the train. She felt much like you, it relaxed her." Smiling, Winston added, "I dare say, she would have very much enjoyed meeting you, Sophie."

"What was her name?"

"Emily. Emily Kathleen…she was not only the most beautiful woman I had ever met…" Grinning, he added, "besides my mother, of course… but she was also a force to be reckoned with." Chuckling, Winston continued, "She was not one to be underestimated and there were many chauvinistic men who found that out the hard way." Winston chuckled as he reminisced. "Something I very much loved about her."

"I would have loved to have met her." Sophie very honestly replied.

"Well, enough of me boring you with conversation. I'm sure you would like some peace and quiet and I think I'll nap before we arrive, otherwise I won't be rested enough to deal with a meeting I have scheduled this afternoon. So, if you will pardon me, Miss Sophie, I will recline my seat and close my eyes."

"Well, it's been lovely speaking with you, Winston. I promise I will be as quiet as a mouse while you sleep." Admittedly, Sophie was getting sleepy herself. The repetitive sound of the train running over the tracks was putting her into an almost trance-like state.

"With thanks." Winston nodded, then proceeded to recline back and go to sleep.

Thankfully he's not a snorer. That would have been very annoying.

Looking across at the man, Sophie couldn't help but notice how handsome he was. He never did say how old he was but if she were to guess she would put him at around seventy, seventy-five, maybe older. It was hard to tell. He was well-built, tall, maybe six feet. Looking at his hand she noticed that he still wore his wedding ring.

What a sweet man.

He appeared to have money given the clothing he was wearing and his mannerisms. Sophie had to admit that she liked him very much.

Putting her head back on the seat, Sophie reclined and closed her eyes.

TWO

WAKING AS THE CONDUCTOR ANNOUNCED their approach to Granite Hill, Sophie checked her watch and noted how the train was arriving as scheduled.

Impressive. You'd be lucky to arrive on time if you were flying.

Seeing Winston was still sleeping, Sophie tried to decide whether to wake him or let the conductor deal with his passenger. Grabbing her purse and carry on luggage, Sophie looked once more at Winston. Tapping him on the arm with no response, she tried once again to waken him. Growing concerned she looked more closely. Checking his wrist, she felt no pulse and immediately hit the emergency button. Dragging him onto the floor, Sophie began CPR.

The conductor arrived and seeing there was a medical emergency immediately radioed for an ambulance to be called so it would be there upon their arrival. He then began clearing the train car of curious individuals, shuffling them along to the next car. Sophie couldn't hear specifically what was being said but she could hear the low muffled voices of those around her.

The whistle screamed, announcing the train's arrival.

Sophie kept working on Winston. The conductor was on his walkie talkie speaking to an unknown individual.

She could hear the steam of the train hissing its discontent as it slowly arrived into the station and then the brakes squealing as the train came to a gentle stop.

Now Winston, I'm telling you right now that you had better fight this. You seem to be one of the good ones and you sure as hell better not die on me!

CPR was physically demanding, however, the adrenaline alone kept her going. She was now more than grateful for the training at work a few years back.

*One, two, three...*she kept counting...*twenty-eight, twenty-nine, thirty.* Leaning in, she gave Winston two rescue breaths then continued with the chest compressions.

"Where the hell is the ambulance?!" She shouted out to anyone who would listen or have an answer.

"They are on their way, Miss. Should be here momentarily." The unknown person shouted. Sophie couldn't see who was speaking and didn't care.

That's right. You get back on that radio of yours and check because by God this man isn't going to die if I have anything to say about it. One, two, three...

She could finally hear sirens in the distance.

Two rescue breaths...C'mon, hurry up! One, two, three...

Sophie could hear a lot of commotion outside. Whoever had answered her about the ambulance was apparently in charge. Hearing whom she assumed were the paramedics board the train, Sophie could hear the gurney trundling along the aisle and felt relief.

"We can take it from here, ma'am."

Reluctantly, Sophie moved out of the way so the paramedics could take over. They had the equipment and the strength that she was quickly losing.

"There is a pulse albeit a faint one. Well done."

Sophie was relieved to hear the good news.

It was tight quarters but they managed to lift Winston up onto the gurney, covered him with a blanket, and strapped him safely in. Sitting down in one of the seats, Sophie was out of breath, suddenly feeling very tired. Laying her head back on the seat she closed her eyes. She needed a minute to catch her breath and gain her strength back.

Opening them again, she noticed Winston's coat and scarf neatly placed over the seat beside where he had sat. Quickly picking them up, Sophie grabbed her belongings, and scrambled off the train towards the ambulance. Seeing them slam the back doors shut she ran up to the one paramedic heading to the driver's door.

"Where are you taking him? Can I go?"

"Are you family?"

"No, I'm not…I'm a friend."

"Then no, you can't go, however, we are taking him to Granite Hill Memorial Hospital. Gotta go."

Watching the paramedic hop into the driver's seat and slam the door shut, Sophie jumped when the sirens suddenly blared and watched as the ambulance sped away.

"Wonderful job, young lady."

Shivering from the chill in the air Sophie turned to see who spoke to her and nodded to the train conductor.

"I have his coat and scarf." She was tired.

"I can take them for you. We will track down who the gentleman is and get them to him at the hospital."

Looking down at the outstretched hand before her, Sophie then looked at Winston's coat and scarf carefully placed over her arm.

"It's okay, I'll take them."

"Oh, he's a friend of yours then?"

Sophie nodded. "Yes, he's a friend."

"Can I get your name and phone number for our records, Miss? In case we need to contact you about anything."

Providing her contact information, Sophie left in search of her rental car.

THREE

ARRIVING AT GRANITE HILL MEMORIAL, Sophie immediately went to the emergency department. Finding the triage nurse she asked for Winston.

"The gentleman who was just brought in here by ambulance. How is he doing?"

"Which gentleman are you referring to? We have many." The nurse seemed bored with her job.

"Older gentleman, grey hair, came from the train station. Winston…"

"Blackburn…" Sophie overheard the nurse mumble to herself.

"I see it right here." Looking at her computer, the nurse offered, "He's in a trauma room right now."

"How is he?" Sophie was anxious to hear.

"Are you family? Friend?" The nurse questioned. "Unless you are family I'm not allowed to disclose any information." The nurse couldn't have looked more disinterested if she tried.

"Of course." Hoping the nurse wouldn't notice she didn't exactly answer her question.

Standing staring at her, Sophie hesitated.

"Well, are you family?" The monotone voice of the nurse echoed through the speaker attached to the very scratched plexiglas divider between them. Receiving no response, the nurse was getting impatient and asked once again, "Are you family?"

"Yes…yes, I'm family. I'm his…daughter."

"Okay, well, he is responding to treatment."

"Does that mean he will make it?" Sophie was hopeful.

"It's not something I can say but right now he is responding well. Once the doctor has a moment, I will have him come speak to you." The nurse turned to her computer and began punching keys before calling for the next patient.

Turning away, Sophie was relieved. At least he was still alive. Finding a seat in the busy waiting area, Sophie sat patiently waiting for the doctor. She felt guilty lying about her relationship with Winston but after what she had been through with him, she wasn't about to just walk away and carry on with her life. That would be nearly impossible now.

Watching as hospital staff came and went to and from various directions, Sophie closed her eyes. She listened to the all too familiar sounds of the hospital. The announcements over the intercom; doctors being summoned to various departments; phones ringing; sirens; the moaning of people waiting to be seen; low muffled conversations; children crying. Then there was that clinical hospital smell that remained the same no matter what hospital you were in.

I wonder why they can't somehow manage to infuse more spa-like smells rather than allowing this antiseptic odour to permeate the halls.

She had dosed off for what seemed like only a few minutes but, as she soon discovered, was well over an hour when she felt a tap on her shoulder.

"Excuse me." The voice quietly awakened her.

Opening her eyes, Sophie looked into the face of a plump, friendly looking, older woman looking very sympathetic and wearing a teal coloured hospital coat with a badge indicating that her name was Gladys, a volunteer at the hospital.

"Yes?" Sophie sat up, wiping the drool from her mouth.

"I can take you to see your father now."

"Oh, he's not my..." Sophie stopped. "Thank you."

Looking around she saw that the waiting room seemed just as busy as it had been an hour earlier but the faces were different. Following Gladys, Sophie was led through a set of doors, down a hall. She walked past trauma room one, two and three each with small windows to see through and all with their doors closed. Approaching trauma room four, Gladys kindly smiled.

"Here you go, my Dear. The doctor is still in with your father. Take care."

Watching Gladys walk back down the hall towards the waiting room, Sophie hesitated before entering. She had come this far with the lies, she might just as well follow through. What was the big deal, anyway? Her intentions were good. After all, she had just saved his life...at least, she hoped she had, and only wanted to be sure he got his coat and scarf.

Pushing through the doors, she hesitated. She was shocked to see the mess of paper and medical litter strewn across the floor. Looking up she could see Winston hooked up to several machines beeping slow, steady beeps. By all indications on the monitor, he was breathing well and his blood pressure seemed stable. That much she could tell, otherwise, she was at a loss.

"Please come in. I'm Doctor Ritchler and you must be his daughter."

"How is he?" Sophie didn't want to get into who she was. She just wanted to be sure he was okay."

"He's doing well. He's stable but he will need surgery to implant a pacemaker. After that, we will know better over the following days but I expect he will make a full recovery."

"Thank goodness." Sophie breathed a sigh of relief.

"He suffered a cardiac arrest…a heart attack. Whoever performed CPR on him saved his life. Had they not started that immediately he would have died. He's lucky."

Sophie was pleased to hear this.

"When will you be performing surgery?"

"They are prepping an operating room now. We will be taking him in very soon but we need some papers signed by you giving us permission to go ahead with the surgery and the possibility of a DNR."

"DNR?"

"Do not resuscitate, should he take a turn for the worse."

"I'm not signing that." Sophie was nervous about getting too involved with the entire situation.

"But I would recommend it." The doctor urged. "Do you have other family you may want to speak to about this? There is still time."

"No…um…yes." Sophie's nerves were getting the best of her. "Do you have his belongings? I'll hang onto them."

"Yes, of course. They are over there on the chair but please discuss this with your family. I'll send a nurse to get you when we need the papers signed."

Leaving the room, Sophie knew she needed to find his family and get them here before he had surgery. They deserved to see him just in case he died during the procedure. Sitting down in the waiting area once again, she opened up his wallet and searched for any sign of family she could call on Winston's behalf.

His driver's license indicated he was actually seventy-six years old and he lived on Primera Lane. Pulling out another card, she was relieved to find an emergency contact card with a name and phone number on it. Given the name on the card, she suspected it might be his son or perhaps a brother.

Pulling out her phone, she dialled the number.

"Hello?" A deep male voice answered.

"Yes, hello. Is this Ethan? Ethan Blackburn?"

"Yes."

"Well, you don't know me but I know Winston."

"Okay, and why are you calling me about my father? I'm quite busy right now."

"Well…"

"Hurry up will you? I've got a meeting I'm expected to be in, with my father, as a matter of fact, not that it's any of your business."

"Well, that's the thing. Your father is in hospital." Sophie stammered over her words. "He's…"

"What?! What happened and why are *you* calling me and not the hospital? And for that matter how did you get my phone number?"

Sophie hesitated unsure of how to respond. She was suddenly feeling very apprehensive.

"You know what? Never mind. What hospital is he at?" Winston's son seemed more angry than worried about his father.

You would think he would ask how his father was? What a jerk he is. Clearly he is nothing like Winston.

"Granite Hill Memorial." Sophie was growing angry.

Hearing the phone hang up, she wasn't looking forward to meeting this son of Winston's. For one thing he was a very rude individual and for another she was concerned about how she was going to explain the fact that she had said she was Winston's daughter? Maybe she wouldn't say anything. He likely wouldn't find out anyway.

FOUR

WITHIN A HALF AN HOUR, a younger, taller version of Winston stormed through the emergency room doors, looking around.

Standing up, Sophie walked towards the man, who finally noticed her then noticed she was carrying his father's coat.

"Was that you who called?" He was in no mood for pleasantries.

"Yes. I'm Sophie..."

"I'll take his things." Ethan abruptly grabbed his father's coat and Sophie handed him the scarf, and other belongings. Grabbing his father's wallet, he immediately began looking through it.

"I certainly hope for your sake that everything is here."

"How dare you?! I would never steal from..."

"Where is he?" Ethan demanded.

"He's in the trauma room..." Sophie was livid and watched in shock as Ethan stormed towards the triage desk demanding to see his father. The nurse quickly obliged and within moments, Gladys the volunteer walked through the doors and indicated for Ethan to follow her.

Sophie watched as Ethan and Gladys disappeared through the doors.

Wow, he's absolutely despicable.

Sophie sat back down. She was so angry right now. She wasn't sure what to do. She had her carry-on suitcase and suddenly remembered her other luggage had been forgotten on the train. She decided it was likely best to wait to speak with Winston's son and once again try to explain what happened, even though she would have preferred not to. She suspected that given his frame of mind, he wouldn't be in the mood to speak with her either. She waited anyway expecting it would be a complete calamity, but felt it was the right thing to do given how Winston ended up here.

A short time later, Ethan stormed back through the doors towards Sophie.

"You told them you were his daughter?!"

"Yes, well...it..."

"How dare you?! What do you think you were doing? What are you up to?" Ethan was furious.

"We were on the train together. I wasn't up to anyth..."

"Are you some gold-digger or something? Trying to take advantage of an old man? What the hell is wrong with you?" His voice echoed throughout the room. People were staring.

Sophie immediately became indignant.

"Excuse me?! How dare you speak to me like that! I was helping your father."

"Oh, I bet you were. By lying? To what end?"

"Sir, I will have to ask you to keep your voice down." The triage nurse was now standing up and leaning out of her cubicle.

Looking behind him, Ethan nodded before lowering his voice.

"Well, you can take your little scheme and leave. You won't be getting a penny out of him. You can be sure I will notify the hospital that you are to go nowhere near him."

Sophie couldn't believe what she was hearing. The man was being completely outrageous, presumptuous and downright offensive. She stood up and grabbed her coat.

"You are unbelievable! I won't stand here and be treated this way. I was only trying to help your father." Turning to leave, Sophie was shaking. Looking back she wanted to say one last thing.

"Your father?"

"What about him?" His words were laced with venom.

"He's a wonderful, kind man."

Seeing Ethan staring condescendingly at her, she added, "And you are nothing like him!"

FIVE

Back at the hotel, Sophie arrived at the front desk, showed her identification and within moments was shown to her suite.

"Is there anything else I can do for you, Ms Callaghan?"

"No, thank you."

"Very well. Have a lovely evening."

Sitting down on one of the chairs in the living room, Sophie suddenly realized she had left her carry-on bag at the hospital and wanted to cry. It had been an emotionally charged day and now she didn't have any of her luggage. Walking into the bedroom she flopped back onto the bed unsure of what to do next. Closing her eyes, she felt exhausted.

Her conversation with Winston's son had upset her but she reminded herself that clearly he was a crass person with absolutely no people skills, whatsoever. He was nothing like his father and she was grateful she would never see him again, although she was disappointed because she would have liked to visit Winston once he was in recovery. She liked him very much.

Looking up the number to the train station, she dialled the number. Thankfully, she was told that they had her luggage in the office and they would have it delivered to her hotel the next day.

As for her carry-on, when she called, she was disappointed to hear that it was not in the waiting room. Letting them know what hotel she was staying at, she hoped they would find her luggage and return it to her but she didn't hold high hopes. Hanging up, she realized that someone had clearly walked away with it. Her day had become a 'shit-show' with no signs of improving anytime soon.

Well, things could be worse. Poor Winston is in hospital likely having heart surgery at this very moment. I suppose I have nothing to complain about.

She was more tired than she was hungry so decided to take a nap before heading out for dinner.

SIX

"Paige, it's Ethan. Dad's in the hospital about to have surgery. I want to be perfectly clear that should some woman call at any point looking for Dad by the name of Sophie, you are under no circumstances to put her through to him. Understood?"

"Yes, absolutely but what's happened with your father?"

Not having the entire story just yet, Ethan could only explain what he knew.

"He had a heart attack and once I speak with Dad, I'll find out exactly what happened but for now, I'll be here at the hospital. Please be sure to cancel all of Dad's appointments for the next couple of weeks until we have further details."

"I'll take care of that right away. Is there anything else I can assist you with, Ethan?"

"No, I'm fine, thank you, Paige. I'll be sure to call the office and have my schedule cleared for the remainder of the week as well."

"I can take care of that for you, if you'd like."

"No, Paige, thank you. You're Dad's personal assistant, not mine, although I appreciate the offer. You'll have enough to do. Listen, I have to go, the doctor is signalling that he wants to speak with me. I'll keep in touch."

"Ethan?"

"Yes?"

"Will he be okay?"

"He should be, Paige. Please don't worry."

Hanging up the phone, Paige *was* extremely worried though. She had worked as Winston's personal assistant for ten years, since she was twenty years old. She adored him and he had always treated her with the utmost respect. He gave her a job when no one else would. She had emigrated from Rwanda with her parents when she was in high school and was unable to continue onto post-secondary right away. Her parents didn't have a lot of money and going to college or university wasn't an option. When she applied for the position of personal assistant, Winston liked her and hired her immediately. He had told her that education wasn't the only element to the job. He had said she seemed to have strength of character and intelligence and he liked her directness. Quite frankly, she was a delight, his words, to be exact.

It wasn't long before Winston found out that Paige was saving to go to university and insisted on paying her tuition. After much argument, she succumbed to his determination to pay and attended part time, eventually graduating with her Business degree. Winston insisted she find another job better aligned with her education but she didn't want to. She was happy working for him. He treated her with kindness and respect and her salary was more than generous. Much more than what she felt she should be making for the job, considering her room and board were also covered. He had even set up a private apartment for her at their home. Paige had grown extremely fond of Winston's wife, Emily, as well, and was devastated when she passed away. Now, hearing that Winston was in hospital after a heart attack was like hearing her own father was in hospital, and she was frankly having a difficult time containing her emotions.

Taking a few moments to compose herself, she picked up the phone and began making calls, clearing Winston's calendar.

SEVEN

WAKING UP, SOPHIE SAW THAT it was dark outside. Checking the time, it was well after midnight. She decided to call to see if room service was still an option. To her disappointment it wasn't. Grabbing her purse, she walked down to the lobby to the coffee shop that was recommended and got herself a salad and an orange.

Walking around the quiet lobby, Sophie reflected back on her day. She wasn't quite as shaken as she had been earlier and wondered how Winston was doing.

Such a nice man. I hope he recovers from this but I suppose I'll never know, thanks to that miserable son of his. How a father and son can be so different is beyond me.

Arriving back at her suite, Sophie turned on the television then sat and ate her salad before heading to bed for the night. Since she didn't have a change of clothes, she undressed, leaving her bra and panties on and crawled into bed.

It took her a few moments to wake up enough to realize someone was knocking at her door.

"Housekeeping."

Trying to shake off the grogginess, Sophie heard another knock at the door.

"Housekeeping."

"I'm good today. Thank you." *I must remember to put the do not disturb sign out next time.*

"Thank you, ma'am."

Lying in bed staring up at the ceiling, she was still quite tired. She hadn't slept well. Her dreams were all about Winston and the events from the day before.

Rolling over, she stared out the window blinking through the sunlight. She had forgotten to close the curtains but she didn't mind. It was rather pleasant lying in the warmth of the sunshine. Looking out at the city skyline and blue skies, Sophie was trying to figure out what to do. Anything but what she was commissioned to do, preferably.

She really didn't want to get out of bed. The feel of the cool sheets on her skin and the softness of the pillows were enough to keep anyone there. Rolling over lying on her back she could hear the rustle of the sheets. They smelled wonderful. She always found a fresh linen smell so comforting.

Another knock at the door shook her out of her morning stupor. Getting out of bed, she threw on a hotel terrycloth robe and trundled to the door. Peeking through the peephole, she saw the bellman and opened the door.

"Yes?"

"I have your luggage, ma'am."

Looking down, Sophie was pleasantly surprised to also see her carry-on suitcase.

"Someone dropped it off at the front desk this morning."

"Who dropped it off?" Sophie was curious.

"I'm not sure. I was only asked to bring both pieces of luggage to your room."

"Here, I'll get you a tip."

"That's not necessary, Ms Callaghan. Thank you."

As he turned to leave, Sophie shouted after him her thanks and shut the door.

"It must have been one of the hospital employees. Possibly that volunteer, Gladys. Regardless, I'm grateful to have both of them."

Opening her carry-on, she was pleased to see it was untouched. Unpacking both suitcases, she carefully put everything away.

Sitting down on the bed, Sophie was trying to decide what to do next when her mobile rang. Seeing who was calling, she reluctantly answered it.

"Hello Francine."

"Sophie. Where are you?"

"Away on vacation."

"You can't just take off like this. You have a job to do."

"I'm not just taking off and I am still doing my job. I've notified everyone at the office that I'll be away on vacation and they can get a hold of me at any time through Tony. The place runs itself. Our parents left everything in good hands with George, our ever reliable COO. As Chief Operating Officer he knows what to do. I completely trust him. Nothing has changed as far as the day-to-day operations go, Francine. The fact that I'm CEO and taking a couple of weeks away for vacation isn't anything to panic about. Tony will let me know if there is anything important that comes up. I can work remotely if necessary."

Getting up, Sophie walked over to the bar fridge and opened it. Looking through it, she was disappointed there was nothing that appealed to her. Grabbing a bottle of water and the orange she bought the night before, she shut the door once again.

"That's not what I mean and you know it. We need to talk. I can help you…we can help you."

"I don't need any help."

"See, now, that's where you're wrong. You must realize that this is far too much for you to deal with on your own, what with your position and having to deal with this…this…nightmare that mother dropped on us. You must see that."

"I really don't see it and that's your opinion, not mine." Sophie appreciated the fresh scent of the orange as she peeled it.

"Not just mine, Tyler's as well."

"Listen Francine, I had a pretty rough day giving some old gentleman CPR yesterday and I'm actually quite tired. I have no interest in discussing this right now."

"You gave an old man CPR?"

"Yes, and quite frankly, I spent a lot of time at a hospital yesterday being yelled at by this guy's son and I don't need to be yelled at by you too. I'm quite capable of dealing with this."

"I don't think you are." Francine insisted.

"Mom and Dad knew I was more than qualified which is why I was designated Mom's successor as Chief Executive Officer and the reason I was named executor of both their wills. The fact that you and Tyler don't think I can is irrelevant. That's what *you* don't understand."

"Regardless of all of that, the more important issue is that they lied to us, Sophie."

"That might be true but these are their…well…Mom's wishes and I plan on executing them once I get back from this trip."

"She wouldn't even know the difference if you didn't…"

"That's a terrible thing to say, Francine, and *I* would know the difference. I could be held personally liable which is another reason why I'm doing what I've been tasked to do." Sophie was adamant.

"Now, Sophie, you know as well as I do that this can't happen. We will take matters further if we have to. We don't want to but we will. Do you really want that hanging over your head?"

"Francine, you and that husband of yours can go to hell."

"You'll regret this."

"I'm pretty sure I won't."

She wasn't entirely sure about that. Her sister could very well be right this time.

"This business belongs to us, no one else."

"No, it really doesn't. Not now, and besides, you are silent partners…"

"This is fucking ridiculous! When you get back I expect you to give us what is rightfully ours! This has gone on long enough, Sophie!"

"You can scream all you want, Francine, but I'm telling you right now that neither you nor Tyler are entitled to one damn thing more than you already received. Just be happy with what you got. Besides, being a silent partner is more than reasonable considering how much you hated the hotel business. I'm in charge now. Not you. Not Tyler. Me. Mom wanted it this way and it's going to be this way."

"Don't you hate her for this? Hate them? All those years of lying to us?"

Sophie noticed that Francine's tone had changed. She was hurt. For that matter, Sophie was hurt too but she knew that what she was doing was right. She also knew that it wasn't their decision to make. It had already been made by their mother.

"I've got to go."

"I mean it, Sophie. We will take matters further if we have to. We will get legal counsel."

"You already have and you lost. It's been almost two years of fighting it. Let it go, Francine, and oh, by the way, the old guy survived."

"What?"

Hanging up on her sister, Sophie was getting tired of having the same conversation over and over again with her.

Francine was several years younger than Sophie. They had never been close, never gotten along. Their personalities and interests were very different. Sophie was always very confident and outgoing whereas Francine was shy and insecure.

The last thing Francine wanted to do was work in the hotel business. Her interests were with acting, something their parents really didn't want her pursuing but, throughout high school, Francine rebelled and they gave in to her hoping it would be a passing phase. Francine's dream was to move to New York City and pursue a career on Broadway. After university, their parents pressured her to give up her misguided vision of becoming an actress and she reluctantly gave in and agreed to work with them.

Sophie on the other hand, was greatly interested in the business and as a result maintained a close relationship with their parents over the years. A relationship Francine resented. Sophie knew her sister had always felt like she needed to claw her way into their parents' 'radar'. Francine grew up at a time when their parents were expanding the business nationally and were struggling as a couple. It was a very tumultuous time, with many arguments and Francine struggled to feel relevant. Sophie understood how heartbreaking it had been for Francine but nothing Sophie could say or do made life any better for her sister.

Once Francine graduated from university, she met Tyler while they were both working for her parents and it was after this that relationships grew even more strained. Tyler fed into Francine's insecurities and did whatever he could to push his agenda, trying to squeeze as much as he could out of the business with less work. Tyler didn't get along with anyone in the family and as a result tensions grew.

Eventually, Francine and Tyler were given roles on the board of directors. Their parents felt the roles could cause little damage but would give them a sense of having some power which they seemed to crave. It didn't go well. In the end, it was recommended Francine and Tyler become silent partners.

When their parents died and they discovered the details of their mother's will, Francine was livid, which didn't make her relationship with Sophie any easier. Sophie dreaded every conversation they had. Their opinions greatly differed on the matter and Sophie could only walk away and let the lawyers deal with Francine and Tyler.

Reflecting back on the conversation with her sister, Sophie knew she needed to distance herself. She was tired of fighting with them every step of the way and she certainly didn't need them figuring out where she was or what she was doing here and possibly interfering. She purposely didn't tell anyone why she was away. She needed to deal with matters under the radar at her own pace.

Turning off the 'find me' app on her phone, she had a revelation and decided it was time for her to get a new number.

Quickly showering and dressing, Sophie grabbed her purse and headed to the nearest mobile phone store. Arranging for a new number, she called the office and gave Tony strict orders not to give the number out to anyone. Then she called the lawyer's office and gave them her new number.

Going for a walk around the downtown core, Sophie felt lost. She wasn't sure how she was going to go through with this.

The whole situation is the most bizarre thing I've ever experienced. Seriously, I just don't get it. How the hell could you not tell us about this, Mom?

This is rather life-altering information, don't you think? I'm having a hard time coming to terms with the entire scenario. I'm nervous and quite frankly, pissed at you both for leaving me to clean up your mess.

Back at the hotel, Sophie was walking through the lobby, which was significantly busier than it had been earlier, when out of the corner of her eye, she saw someone stand up. Glancing over, she was shocked at who she saw. Stopping in her tracks, she prepared for the worst.

EIGHT

"WHAT DO *YOU* WANT?" SHE was instantly irritated just by the sight of him.

"Can we talk?" Ethan asked quietly.

"Why?"

"Please...sit." Indicating the chair beside him, Ethan waited.

"Why would I even want to?" Sophie was cautious.

"I owe you an apology."

Sophie was surprised to hear his confession.

"This is true." She stood with her arms crossed in front of her.

"My father explained who you were."

Staring at him with a look of indifference, Sophie asked, "And how is he?"

"He's doing well. He's going to make a full recovery. They implanted a pacemaker last night and he should live a very long life. He will be out of hospital by the weekend."

"I'm very happy to hear that." Sophie remained indifferent but meant what she said.

"He was upset with me..."

The awkwardness was evident. The man seemingly wasn't used to having to apologize as far as Sophie could figure.

"Really."

"Very." Ethan fidgeted under Sophie's judging eyes.

"Glad to hear that."

"I also found out through the train conductor that a young lady sitting across from my father had saved his life. He didn't give me a name due to privacy but…"

"Is that right?" Sophie couldn't help her sarcasm.

"That was you."

"Yes." She was less than interested in hearing about his revelation.

Nodding his head, Ethan looked extremely uncomfortable.

"Thank you."

Sophie said nothing.

"I was completely out of line…"

"You were."

"And I apologize."

Standing, staring coldly in his direction, Sophie didn't respond.

"You didn't deserve how I treated you. I said some pretty terrible things…"

"You did." Sophie wasn't about to let him off the hook.

"There was no excuse."

"True."

"My father sent me here to apologize."

"You needed your father to tell you to come and apologize?"

"No! No! Not at all. Let's just say he made it perfectly clear…" Ethan sighed, thinking carefully about what he should say next.

"Listen…I was wondering if I could interest you in dinner tonight? It's the least I can do."

"With you?" Sophie's eyebrows raised in surprise.

"Yes."

"Was this your father's idea?"

"No, it was all mine."

"Why would I want to after the way you treated me?"

Nodding, Ethan didn't really have a response to her question.

"I suppose you shouldn't…want to, that is, but I was hoping you would."

"Do you think a dinner can make up for what you accused me of?" Sophie wasn't entirely sure she wanted to go.

"Yes."

"Yes??"

"Maybe?" Flustered, Ethan wasn't sure what the right answer was.

Sophie found it rather entertaining watching him squirm. He deserved to.

"Are you going to yell at me?" She wanted to know.

"No."

"Are you going to accuse me of being a gold-digger when you pay for the bill?"

"No." This was rather cringeworthy for Ethan. Apologizing wasn't his strong suit. "…I'm sorry, sincerely."

"Are you going to accuse me of taking advantage of an old man?"

"I'm not *that* old…" Ethan stopped speaking when he saw Sophie's disapproving look.

"You're certainly much older than me and I might add, old enough to know how *not* to behave."

Ethan knew enough to keep quiet. He stood there feeling like he was being scolded by his mother…a much younger version, mind you. Truth be told, he found her to be very attractive. She appeared to be maybe five foot eight or nine, wavy auburn hair that fell just below her shoulders, nice figure and, very likely, green eyes although he couldn't tell because of the way she was frowning at him at that very moment.

Thinking for a few minutes, Sophie asked, "And where might this dinner be? That is…if I were to go."

"Where would you like to go?" Ethan felt some relief knowing he might be able to redeem himself and that she was considering dinner with him.

"Where did you have in mind?" Sophie was curious.

"I thought of Frigo's. It's the best place in town and by far the hardest to get into." Ethan was hoping this would entice Sophie.

"I don't have anything fancy to wear."

"Okay, so wherever you would like to go. You name it and we will go." Ethan figured there weren't too many restaurants in Granite Hill that he didn't like. It was a pretty safe bet to let Sophie choose.

"Remind me, how far away from the ocean are we?"

"Perhaps, fifty kilometers. Why?"

"Then I have the perfect idea for dinner tonight and we can both dress casual. You do know how to dress casually don't you? I mean that fancy suit just won't cut it where we are going."

"I can dress casual, yes." Ethan looked down at his suit and gave it a brush with his hands wiping off nothing in particular.

"Then you can pick me up by three." Turning to walk away, Sophie stopped and turned to see that Ethan hadn't moved from where he was standing. "Oh, and bring a *very* expensive bottle of wine with you and some glasses. It's the least you can do."

The look of awkwardness and surprise on Ethan's face was enough to satisfy her need for payback.

Turning to walk away again, she proceeded to walk right into an older woman and just about knocked her over. After apologizing, Sophie walked away, disappointed she hadn't left in the dignified manner she had planned but didn't dare look back. Keeping her head held high she just hoped and prayed that Ethan hadn't been watching.

Going up the elevator back to her suite, she smiled.

He's a very good looking man and my God that cologne he wears is intoxicating.

NINE

"Not only are you prompt but, I see, you really can dress down. Well done." Sophie teased, looking at his jeans and crewneck sweater. "So, do you have the wine?"

Opening the door of his car, Ethan waited for Sophie to get in, "Yes, I have the wine. Is that the only reason you came?"

"Pretty much," she grinned.

"And for your information, I don't always wear suits. You do realize that today is a business day. A suit is appropriate."

She was thankful for her choice of venue for dinner. She was by far more comfortable in the jeans and sweatshirt she had on than any business suit she had to wear these days. Sneakers were also a welcome relief from stilettos.

Getting into the car, Ethan asked, "So, where are we going?"

"Do you know where Porter's Pier is?"

"Of course."

Less than an hour later, they pulled up in front of a small wooden shack-style building with a rustic sign over the door that read, 'Larry's Lobster Shack'.

Getting out of the car, Sophie and Ethan walked up and into the shack. It was very rustic inside and simplistic, to say the least, with a strong fishy odour permeating throughout. There was one counter with a tank on top loaded with lobsters climbing all over each other. Behind that there was a refrigerator, a small counter and some shelving with platters and glasses neatly stacked.

"Well, hello there! How can I help ya? I'm Norm of said Larry's Lobster Shack and all these here beauties were fresh caught this mornin'. You pick 'em, we cook 'em with your choice of salad and some good ole garlic butter for dippin'."

Smiling, Sophie pointed to the lobster she wanted, with Ethan choosing his next.

"I'll get 'em cooked up for ya and bring them straight away. Can I get ya a drink? We have water, beer and soda pop."

"No, thank you, we brought our own." Ethan opened the door for Sophie and followed her out to a picnic table near the water.

"This is so picturesque don't you think?" Sophie was mesmerized by the small harbour filled with various coloured fishing boats all bobbing with the waves on the sun sparkled water. Some were tied to docks, others to another boat. The autumn leaves on the trees reflecting onto the water added to the overall beauty.

"It is. I haven't been out here since I was a kid."

"So you know this place then?" Sophie sat down.

Following suit, Ethan, smiled. "Very much so. My father used to bring me here from time to time when I was a kid. It wasn't owned by Norm back then. His father Larry owned it but I can assure you that it hasn't changed a bit. He and my father were business acquaintances."

"I think the meal here will be better than any restaurant we could've gone to." Sophie couldn't be absolutely sure but there was no one who could convince her that fresh lobster caught that morning could be beat.

Taking in a deep breath, she closed her eyes as she took in the smell of the ocean air infused with the unmistakable smell of fish and seaweed. Not a pleasant smell to most but to Sophie it took her back to the days when her family would vacation on the East Coast in the summer. She used to love fishing, going boating but mostly swimming and lying on the beach, slathered in coconut scented sunscreen, on a cozy towel in the hot sun. Those were the days.

The breeze picked up and she shivered from the chilly air.

"Cold?"

"Just a bit chilly. I'll get my jacket from the car."

"I'll get it. Be right back." Ethan stood up and left her sitting staring out at the water and the lighthouse in the distance.

"Here ya go, little lady. Fresh lobster and salad." Placing the tray on the table in front of Sophie, Norm hurried back into the shack, returning moments later with another tray which he placed on the table across from her, then left as quickly as he had appeared.

Ethan returned with Sophie's jacket in one hand and wine and glasses in the other. Smiling when he saw the tray of lobster presented before him, he quickly sat down. Opening the bottle of wine, he poured them each a glass.

"Cheers! To forgiveness." He smiled hopefully at Sophie.

Grinning, she nodded, "Cheers!" Tapping her glass gently against his, she added, "To forgiveness."

Ethan took a sip of his wine. "Now, let's eat."

TEN

Sophie removed her lobster bib and placed it on the plate. "Oh my God, that was delicious! I haven't had lobster in years."

"I must admit, this was a great choice for dinner." Ethan couldn't deny that this was a much better option than Frigo's.

"I was hoping you might think so." Sitting quietly for a moment sipping on her wine, Sophie asked, "So how is your dad? Did you speak to him this afternoon?"

"Yes, absolutely. He's doing great. He was starting to complain about the food, insisting it was time to go home. I feel sorry for the nurses. He's a hard man to hold down."

"I could see that in him." Sophie grinned.

"You saved his life and words can't express how grateful I am to you for that." Ethan's sincerity was evident. "You have no idea…"

"Oh, I think I do and you're welcome."

Sitting quietly for a few moments, Ethan cleared his throat.

"Listen, I really must say once again how truly sorry I am for my behaviour at the hospital yesterday. There really was no excuse…"

"Would you relax? You already apologized and now you've treated me to dinner and some pretty great wine. I think I can forgive your abhorrent behaviour."

"Abhorrent? A bit harsh wouldn't you say?"

"Hmmm…no, I think it's a pretty accurate description." Smiling, Sophie's eyes lingered a few moments longer on Ethan before he caught her staring.

He's an interesting person. He seems to be a nice guy. After his behaviour last night I would have pegged him as one of the biggest assholes I'd ever met but today he seems like a somewhat decent person…even likeable. And it doesn't hurt that he's wearing that incredible cologne again.

"So, what brings you to Granite Hill?" Ethan was curious about this woman who happened upon his path so unexpectedly.

"Family." Again, Sophie didn't want to elaborate and kept it simple.

"I see, but not family you could stay with?"

"No, not family I can stay with." She was purposely being reticent about her personal life. She wasn't sure what to make of it herself these days.

Listening to the seagulls squeal, she watched as one plunged into the water, quickly coming back up with a fish in its mouth.

Sophie wasn't sure where to go with the conversation. It felt awkward considering they really didn't know each other. "Shall we go for a walk? Work off this dinner?"

"There is a beach just down the road if you're interested."

"I am very interested," she smiled.

Arriving at the beach, Sophie noticed there were very few people walking around. She reminded herself that it was, after all, early October with a bit of a chill in the air.

Walking along the beach, Sophie relaxed immediately.

"I haven't walked a beach in years. We used to go east for our summer vacations and I have fond memories of walking the beach there with my parents and sister, splashing our feet in the water as the waves washed in, the wet sand under our feet."

"Sounds nice. I can't say that we did that as a family. However, I did spend much of my university years at the beach with friends, swimming, surfing. Always fun times."

Ethan smiled thinking back to his younger, more carefree days, and friends he rarely got to see anymore. Life had just become too busy in recent years and especially in the last several months. He had let friendships slip through the cracks, something he greatly regretted and hoped to rectify one day soon.

Finding a log to sit down on, they sat quietly enjoying the view. Sophie was mesmerized watching the ocean waves envelop the sand each time they washed along the shoreline. Someone had built a sand castle that was barely holding its own against the encroaching waves. Staring out at the beautiful sunset that was blossoming into orange, yellow and red hues of fiery beauty, Sophie closed her eyes, enjoying the feel of the cool breeze off the water gently brushing through her hair.

Ethan couldn't take his eyes off Sophie, wondering more about her.

"How long will you be staying in Granite Hill?"

Ethan removed his sneakers and socks then placed them beside him. Rolling up his jeans above his ankles, he stretched his legs out, scrunching his toes into the very cool sand. He had to admit to himself that it was just a tad cool for bare feet but he persevered. It had been a long time since he had just kicked back and spent some time at the beach. He missed it.

"I'm not sure."

Sophie truthfully wasn't in a hurry to return home given her many conversations with Francine. She hadn't asked to be executor, but she was and she planned on following through with her mother's wishes to the best of her ability, whether Francine and Tyler liked it or not. To say she was shocked by her mother's will was an understatement. It took her months to process what had been disclosed. Months of emotional turmoil over it all, and the legal battle that Francine and Tyler put up had been exhausting.

"Are you staying at a hotel the entire time? That could get expensive. I have connections…"

"No, it's fine, thank you. I'm used to it. I'm trying to work out the details right now and, until I do, I won't know how long I will be here." She felt rather lost when it came to her own family at the moment. She knew it would take some time.

"So, Ethan, what do you do for a living?"

Sophie was interested to know what made this man tick. Glancing over at him, she came to the conclusion that he was indeed very handsome with a fit physique, approximately six foot two or three, give or take, deep brown eyes, his brown hair, slightly ruffled by the wind had that salt and pepper look starting to appear, like his father.

"Family run business. Nothing too exciting. I don't like talking about work really. It has always sent my dates running."

"Dates?" Sophie's eyes grew large with interest.

"Well, not that we are on a date…what I mean is…when I *was* on a date with a woman…not that you aren't a woman…"

"I'm glad you noticed." Sophie laughed.

"Oh, I noticed."

"Well, thank you." Sophie chuckled.

He hadn't intended on saying that out loud. Feeling a little awkward by his response, Ethan tried to redirect the conversation, and asked, "How about you?"

"What?"

"What do you do for a living?"

"Same. Family business" Sophie sat quietly for a few moments. "So, are you married? Kids?" Looking over at Ethan, she grinned, "Grandkids?"

Flashing a resentful look in her direction, Ethan asked, "So you think I'm much older than you, do you?"

Looking at him, she nodded and smiled. "I think you likely are, yes."

"Really? And how old do you think I am?"

"I would guess around fifty, early fifties, give or take."

"Ow. That hurts."

"How old are you then?"

"Forty-seven. You were close," he seemed perplexed that she had been so accurate.

"As I said, a decade older than me. I'd say that's pretty old."

"Thirty-seven! I would have pegged you in your mid forties."

"Hurtful!" Sophie laughed seeing that he wasn't serious.

"So, how about you? Married? Kids? I suppose you are too young for grandkids. Boyfriend perhaps?" He was very curious to find out whether she had a significant other.

"Definitely no boyfriend and yes, I'm definitely too young for grandkids. Not married, no kids. Not in the cards for me, I suppose."

"You're still young. Lots of time." Ethan reassured her.

"So they say." Sophie watched as a fishing boat slowly motored past them, most likely towards the harbour. "I'm not particularly concerned about getting married. I was when I was younger but now…not so much. I'm pretty happy where I am in life right now."

Ethan nodded his acknowledgement.

Sophie, you are such a liar! When was the last time you had any fun?

Thinking for a moment, she grew perplexed.

My God! When was the last time I even had sex? Not that I necessarily want to be married but jeez, a little sex wouldn't hurt. My life has been a bloody mishmash of sad and pathetic for a couple of years now.

Shaking off the frustration she was feeling with her life, Sophie changed the subject.

"I must say, your father is a lovely man…very handsome. It was so nice to meet him. You look much like him."

"Oh, I do, do I?"

Sophie blushed realizing what she had implied.

Ignoring his comment, Sophie continued, "We had quite a nice conversation on the train until he scared the life out of me. Yesterday, is not a day I care to repeat anytime soon. Be sure to tell him I say hello and wish him well."

"You can tell him yourself. He's asked to see you."

"He has?" Sophie was surprised by this. "That's very sweet but I'm sure he should rest. I'm not family and to be honest, I'm a bit embarrassed to set foot in that hospital again. I did lie to the nurses and doctor after all and well, I don't particularly want to show up there only to be kicked back out again."

Ethan cringed understanding the role he had played that night.

"Actually, he gets home on Thursday. Why don't you come to the house on Saturday to see him? He would like that I'm sure."

"He'll be exhausted when he first gets home. No, I'm sure he has more important people to see than me." Sophie felt uncomfortable.

"For someone who so altruistically saved his life, I'm sure there is no one more important for him to see right now." Ethan grew serious.

Looking at him, Sophie bit down on her bottom lip. "I'm sure anyone would have done the same. I just happened to be in the right place at the right time."

"Perhaps." Ethan thought about what he was going to say next. "But *you* are the one who saved him and *you* are the one he seems to have taken a liking to, although I'm not sure why," he grinned.

"Gee thanks!"

Ethan laughed. "Seriously though, he really wants to see you."

Sophie was touched by the sentiment. She had taken a liking to Winston as well and admittedly, she really wanted to see him again. He reminded her very much of her father.

"I suppose I could as long as you're sure it won't be too much for him."

"I'm sure, and trust me, he's tenacious about what he wants and he wants to see you."

Nodding, Sophie looked out over the ocean enjoying the sound of the waves washing along the shoreline.

It wasn't long before the sun had disappeared below the horizon. Stars began peeking through the twilight, one by one, like tiny little lights, while the reflection of the full moon shone brightly across the water. The breeze softly brushed across Sophie's face, blowing her hair gently as it did and encouraging goosebumps to appear on her skin. The waves washing along the shoreline were hypnotizing. The moment was picture perfect as far as she was concerned.

"Did you want to get going?" Ethan asked.

"Do you mind if we stay a bit longer?" Sophie felt more relaxed here with a virtual stranger on this sandy beach than she had at home recently.

"Well, I suppose we could." Ethan brushed the sand off his feet. He couldn't ignore that it really was just too cold to go barefoot.

Watching him put his socks and shoes on and hearing what she took as reluctance in Ethan's voice, Sophie reconsidered her request.

"I'm sorry, I really shouldn't be monopolizing your time like this. You must have a million other things you should be doing rather than catering to me." Sophie stood up and reached for her purse.

"No. It's fine."

"Are you sure?"

"Yes, absolutely." In fact, for Ethan, it was more than fine. He was actually quite surprised at how much he was enjoying himself. Sitting on the beach was one of his guilty pleasures. He hadn't taken the time to do this or just enjoy life and unwind in a very long time. Not to mention, being with a beautiful woman at the same time certainly added to the enjoyment of the moment.

Sophie relaxed, confident he was the type of person who would say what he meant. Sitting back down once again she shivered from the cool breeze.

"You don't happen to have a blanket in your car do you? I'm getting a bit chilly."

"I'm pretty sure I do. I'll be right back."

Returning with a blanket, Sophie was surprised when he opened it up and gently placed it across her shoulders and patted them gently before sitting back down.

"There, that should help."

"Oh, um…thank you."

She couldn't help but melt just a little bit by the small but kind gesture. Catching a whiff of his cologne she closed her eyes in appreciation.

"I even found some matches in the glovebox. I'll start a fire."

Gathering driftwood, Ethan dug a hole in the sand and strategically placed the wood for optimal burning. It wasn't long before there was a warm, crackling fire for them to enjoy.

"So, Ethan, tell me more about you and your dad. Are you an only child? I know your mom died and I'm very sorry."

"Thank you. Well, there isn't much to say, really. Right now there is just dad and I..." Ethan stopped talking, unsure of whether he'd wanted to divulge much more about recent events to someone he just met regardless of how comfortable he was feeling with her.

Noticing his hesitation, Sophie said, "Listen, I'm sorry. I didn't mean to pry."

"Really, it's okay."

Sophie wasn't quite sure what else to talk about. It suddenly felt very awkward.

"What about you? What do you like to do for fun?" Ethan poked at the fire as sparks danced up with the smoke into the night sky.

"I don't know. I've been too busy lately to have much fun if you want to know the truth. I used to love to travel, go to baseball games, but have had no time these last couple of years. Maybe one day again soon."

"Travelling and baseball are always fun. Why no time?"

"Well, my parents died a couple of years ago and I've had to get more involved in the family business."

"Ah, yes. Family loyalty. Always a price to pay, although I am sorry to hear about your parents."

"Thank you and yes, I suppose you're right. You would understand, being involved with a family business yourself." Sophie poked at the fire with a stick. "Do you ever get time just for yourself? Time to relax?"

"Not as much as I once did."

"Well, I suppose it's good we have tonight then. We could both use the downtime."

Ethan quietly concurred.

ELEVEN

CHECKING THE TIME, SOPHIE WAS shocked to see it was almost ten o'clock.

"Oh, my goodness. I guess we should be going. I'm sorry to have kept you so long. You have work tomorrow." Sophie stood up and brushed the sand off herself.

"I don't have work tomorrow. I've taken the rest of the week off. That way I can visit dad at the hospital and then bring him home on Thursday, but I suppose you're right, it is getting cold."

"It was a lovely evening. Truly, I haven't taken time out like this for as long as I can remember."

"It's the least I could do." Throwing sand on top of the fire to extinguish it, Ethan grabbed the blanket and gave it a shake, then brushed himself off.

"Well, I certainly hope you didn't feel obligated…"

"Not what I meant at all."

Driving home, Sophie felt surprisingly disappointed the evening was ending. There was something about Ethan that she couldn't explain. Something that uncharacteristically attracted her to him, and so quickly. He had a calmness about him that captivated her, which was surprising, considering how they'd met. He was a bit mysterious, very confident and he seemed to have strength of character, although she didn't know him well enough to make that assessment quite yet. It was just her intuition. He was certainly a bit of a badass, yet there was a hidden gentleness about him.

"Hey, would you like to grab a coffee?" Sophie was hopeful.

"I could stand a coffee, yes, and I know the perfect place."

In no time at all, they were back in the city and Ethan pulled up across the street from a small café. Sophie thought it was quite pretty on the outside with barn board covering the exterior walls. It was brightly lit with strings of white lights criss-crossing from one end of the busy patio to the other. There were tall heaters outside allowing those who chose, to sit outside, and enjoy the cool evening. Looking up, Sophie noticed the name of the coffee shop, Café de Phil.

"This is my 'go to' coffee shop. A buddy of mine from university is the owner and I try to support him as much as possible when I'm in the area. C'mon in."

"I take it Phil is your buddy?" Sophie asked.

"Yes, that he is." Ethan laughed.

Following Ethan inside, Sophie was amazed at how busy it was considering the day of the week and time of night. She certainly didn't expect to see it completely full inside and out.

"Sophie, what would you like to drink?"

"I'll take a chai tea latte, please."

Waiting while Ethan placed the order, Sophie looked around and admired how quaint the place was - wood plank walls, metal signs on the walls with various coffee quotes or pictures related to tea, coffee or anything else a coffee shop might serve. There were strings of lights everywhere giving off a warm glow throughout. She could hear the whir of the coffee machine as it worked and the clattering of cups and plates. The wonderful aroma of coffee filled the air. Some patrons were quietly talking amongst themselves, others were sitting wearing ear buds working away on their laptops. There was a fireplace roaring in the middle of the room. The atmosphere was serene and welcoming.

"Here you go. I think that table is free now." Pointing towards a table by the fireplace, Ethan followed closely behind Sophie and placed both drinks on the table before sitting. Taking a seat, Sophie appreciated the warmth the fire offered on a cool evening.

"This is a wonderful place, Ethan. I can understand why it's so busy here."

"I would hold your praise until you try the latte." Ethan joked.

Sophie laughed and took a sip.

"This is fabulous! The best I've ever had!" She was very impressed.

"Phil has spent years perfecting all of his drinks. He took the time to find the right coffee and tea suppliers, all free trade. He uses local dairies and all his baked goods are made right here on site. He hired top notch people to create one of a kind pastries and baked goods. He really is a perfectionist and it has proven to be a successful strategy."

"I would agree, just looking around and seeing how busy he is, it seems to have paid off."

"One second." With that, Ethan, got up and walked over to the counter returning moments later with a plate filled with several smaller sized pastries.

"You have to try these."

Sharing them, Sophie couldn't believe how delicious they all were.

"Oh my God, Ethan. These really are amazing!"

They spent much time talking and laughing before Sophie looked up at the clock on the wall and saw that it was almost twelve-thirty.

"I suppose we should get going. It was a crazy day yesterday. I think I need to catch up on my sleep. Admittedly, I'm quite tired and I'm sure this place must close soon."

"They close at one o'clock but I agree, let's head out."

Ethan waved good-bye to whom Sophie assumed must be Phil and they headed out the door.

"Here you go, home safe and sound and I didn't even yell at you." Ethan announced as he got out of the car to open her door.

"And I thank you for that." Sophie laughed.

Ethan wouldn't have admitted it but he really did have one of the best evenings in a very long time. There was something about Sophie that he couldn't quite place but he found himself surprisingly attracted to her.

Sophie hesitated before turning to walk away. "Ethan?"

"Yes?"

"Thank you for dinner and the wonderful evening. It's the most fun I've had in quite a while."

"You're most welcome and thank you for allowing me to redeem myself."

Sophie chuckled as Ethan did a half bow in her direction.

"I'll pick you up on Saturday. Would noon work for you? I thought you could spend some time visiting dad, he could have a nap, then we could do dinner together at home. How does that sound?"

"Perfect, but you don't have to pick me up. I don't mind driving myself. I have a rental."

"It's no trouble at all. See you then." Getting into his car, Ethan lowered the passenger window and shouted, "By the way, I can see why my father likes you so much." Waving good-bye, he left a speechless Sophie staring at his tail lights as he drove away.

Sophie couldn't help but break into a big smile.

I have to admit, I really like the guy. Who would have thought?

TWELVE

THE NEXT DAY, SOPHIE STRUGGLED with making the difficult phone call that she knew needed to be made. She was nervous. In the long run, she didn't know what kind of a reaction she would get to the news she was about to deliver. Lying in bed, she pondered the thought of just letting Francine and Tyler deal with this.

God knows it would be so much easier for me. Mom, why did you do this to me? Why did you do this to us? For that matter, how did you keep it a secret for so long? I don't know why I don't hate you and dad right now for lying to us all these years. I was angry at you both for so long but now I just don't know how to feel.

Showering and dressing, Sophie checked in with Tony before heading down to the hotel restaurant for breakfast.

"How are things going? Have Francine and Tyler been hounding you?" Sophie expected she knew the answer to her own question.

"Of course they have. Are you surprised?"

"Not in the least. Just stay strong, Tony. I need time and you're the man to get it for me. Where would I be without you?"

"Oh, stop with your pathetic manipulation. You think I can't see through that? You're terrible at it," he teased.

"Okay, okay." Sophie laughed. "But seriously, Tony, you know what they can be like."

"Do I ever, but not to worry, I'm dealing with them and their relentless pestering."

"You're the best! I'll call you in a few days."

Hanging up, Sophie headed down for breakfast.

"Right this way, Ms Callaghan. Your table is waiting for you. It's been some time since you were here last."

"Yes, well, my parents…" She hesitated.

"I'm very sorry to hear of your parents' passing. They were remarkable people."

"Thank you." Sitting down she picked up a menu and started to look through it.

"May I get you coffee to start?"

"A bloody Caesar please, Marvin, thank you."

"Oh, well, you see…"

"Yes?"

"You see, Ms Callaghan, the bar isn't open just yet. However, I could see…"

"No, not necessary. Coffee will be fine, thank you." Sophie had grabbed a newspaper and glanced through it as she waited for her coffee that arrived moments later.

"Here you go."

"Thank you and I would like the eggs Benedict this morning with a small grapefruit juice."

"Right away." Marvin turned and quickly headed towards the kitchen.

"Ms Callaghan, how nice to see you."

Sophie heard a familiar voice. Looking around, she stood up and smiled. "Anika, how are you?" Leaning in, Sophie gave the woman a hug before sitting down once again. "Please, won't you join me."

"Thank you, but only for a moment. I have a management meeting shortly. I am sorry about the loss of your parents. I understood they wanted a small memorial, family only?"

"Yes, as you know, they were never ones for a big fuss or anything too splashy."

"And Francine? She was satisfied with that?"

"No, but I'm sure that doesn't surprise you."

Anika smiled.

"What brings you to Granite Hill? Will you be staying long?"

"I have some personal matters to attend to. I'm not sure how long I'll be staying."

Sophie liked Anika very much. She was hotel manager of the C-Granite Hotel with oversight of five others throughout the extended region and there was no one more competent than she was. She started working at the hotel when she had arrived from India and never left, making her way up the ranks. She ran a tight but fair ship.

Anika was a very compassionate woman, who once made the decision to allow a refugee family fleeing their country to stay in one of the hotel's finest suites for a few weeks, gratis, until they were able to move into their permanent home. There was a lot of controversy over that, mostly from Francine and Tyler, who sat on the board of directors at the time. They found the decision to be completely irresponsible, concerned that the well to do customers would be uncomfortable; that the place could possibly be blown up; or more importantly, about the thousands in lost revenue. Thankfully, Anika stood her ground, with support from the rest of the board, citing any of their concerns as being unwarranted.

Years later, when the hotel had a widely publicized legal case to contend with, Anika was surprised to have Mr. Kabongo, the father of said refugee family, appear in her office offering his legal services. She was soon to discover that he had been a top litigation lawyer back home and was now able to practice in this country. It became a yearslong case which they eventually won, thanks to Mr. Kabongo, who refused to take a penny for his services. In his words, 'it is with much gratitude from my family'.

Much to Francine and Tyler's chagrin, Anika gave the family a VIP hotel pass that allowed them to stay free of charge at any of the six hotels that she oversaw.

"But we don't have VIP hotel passes for our 'C' line of hotels Granite, Royal, Cypress…or…or any of our hotel lines, for that matter." Francine was livid. "What the hell does Anika think she's doing? She's going to cost us a fortune in lost revenue!"

"She needs to be fired. She has poor judgement. We've all seen that over the years." Tyler pleaded with the board of directors.

The board voted against Francine and Tyler's recommendations and soon after, they resigned from the board.

Drawing herself back to her conversation with Anika, Sophie wasn't sure how to answer the question.

"Once I'm done here, I'm supposed to just head back home to Cedardale but it depends on how things go here."

"Well, it's nice that you visit us periodically. We are always happy to see you. Remind me, how long has it been since you worked here?"

"Twelve years and I remember those years very well. They were some of the best years of my life."

"You did very well. You learned everything from the ground up."

"Yes, as father insisted…if I want to take over the business one day, I need to learn about it all."

"And you did." Anika smiled.

Sitting quietly thinking for a moment, Sophie laughed, "Laundry was an interesting time."

"Ah, but such an important aspect of running any hotel. Without laundry, we wouldn't be in operation." Anika's philosophy was that no job was more important than the next, which is why she made such a phenomenal hotel manager.

"This is very true." Sophie smiled. "Didn't you start with the hotel just before I came to work here?"

"Yes, three years prior."

"That's right, I remember now."

"Your breakfast." Sophie was pleased to see Marvin place her plate of eggs Benedict down in front of her.

"Thank you, Marvin."

"My pleasure." Looking towards Anika, Marvin gave a nod in her direction then left.

Anika stood up. "Enjoy your breakfast. I'm sure I'll see you again during your stay here. Nice to see you, Sophie."

"Nice to see you as well, Anika."

THIRTEEN

Sophie spent all week mulling over how to approach things. She was anxious about dealing with her mother's will. She hadn't even made the phone call that was so crucial to starting the process. She was purposely procrastinating.

What the hell will this person think of me...of us...of the whole situation? I'm sure they will have no clue any more than we did. How will they react? God knows I was shocked...and angry...we all were, so I'm sure they will be too.

Mom, why in hell couldn't you have given us all a bit of a heads up? This shocking movie-style reading of the will was completely unnecessary. You know that Francine is really angry with you right now, well, at both of you.

Yes, I suppose you do know.

The days had dragged on but by Thursday morning she finally gathered the nerve and dialled the number that had been in the letter.

Please don't pick up. Please don't pick up.

"Good morning. Maison, McIlroy, and Hawthorne Law Firm, how may I help you?"

The monotone voice at the other end of the phone waited patiently for a response.

Shit!

Hearing the young man's voice was more than Sophie could take and she immediately hung up.

Okay, I can't do this right now. Maybe later.

She knew that the moment she made that phone call, the ball would start rolling and things would no longer be in her control. She was nervous.

Grabbing her purse she headed out for a walk. She knew she had to pick up something for Winston on Saturday and decided to distract herself with this small but necessary task. At first, she thought wine might be a good idea.

Oops, that won't work for a heart patient just coming home. No sweets either...hmmm...

Walking past a florist she opted for a pot of mixed plants, deciding that the wine would still be included but for herself and Ethan to enjoy. Walking into the flower shop she was instantly enveloped by a glorious essence. She tried to imagine which flowers she was smelling. She immediately walked over and into the floral fridge. The various colours were absolutely stunning. The pink carnations, purple Peruvian lilies, red roses, orange day lilies, white baby's breath, yellow daisies and the various coloured tulips were gorgeous. It was a sight to behold and such a welcoming aroma. It took Sophie back to when she helped her mother with their gardens as a little girl.

"May I help you?"

Sophie was pulled from her thoughts and turned to see a kind looking older woman wearing an apron, smiling at her.

"I was admiring your flowers. They are so beautiful."

"Thank you and yes, I never get tired of looking at them myself."

"I'm sure." Sophie glanced back at the flowers then stepping out of the fridge she answered. "I was hoping to get a pot filled with various plants for an older gentleman."

"Of course, and did you want to pick them out yourself?"

"No, that's fine. I'll trust your best judgement."

"Very well, and when would you like to pick it up or would you like it delivered?" The woman was writing the information down as they spoke.

"I'll be by to pick it up on Saturday morning. Thank you so much."

Leaving the shop, Sophie continued walking until she reached Maple Park. Finding a bench, she sat down and enjoyed the warm sunshine and gentle breeze that had picked up. Closing her eyes, she smiled, hearing birds chirping and leaves rustling in the breeze as they fell to the ground. She could hear people quietly talking, laughter from children. It wasn't long before she heard a child start to cry and a father quickly consoling him/her. Opening her eyes again, she just sat and watched as people walked or ran by with their children or dogs. She remembered the days her father would take her and Francine to the park back home. They were fun days, carefree days.

Sitting there, she realized how retrospective she had been feeling lately. She missed her parents very much, today, more than ever, and it likely had a lot to do with her task at hand. She felt apprehensive at the thought of phoning again. She was terrified about how life was going to change moving forward after this, and she was reluctant to take the next step towards that change.

FOURTEEN

FRIDAY MORNING ARRIVED AND SOPHIE was still hesitant to make the phone call. Trying to put it out of her mind, she went for a walk after breakfast. She loved walking downtown in Granite Hill. It was so beautiful with the mountains and the fresh air. It was busy but the city was small enough that it had a more relaxed feel to it than Cedardale, a city ten times the population of Granite Hill. People didn't hustle and bustle here like they did back home.

Surprised to hear her phone ring, she smiled as she answered. There were only three people she had given the number to.

"Ethan, how are you today?"

"I'm well."

"How is your father?"

"He's very well. He was released from the hospital yesterday and I must say he was pleased to learn you were coming by tomorrow."

"Ah well, that's very sweet of you to say." Sophie was humbled by the sentiment.

"I was calling to ask if you had any plans today?"

"Not at the moment. Why do you ask?"

"I wondered if you would like to join me this afternoon?"

"Doing what?" Sophie was curious.

"I'd rather not say. Just wanted to show you something I thought you might enjoy. Trying to take some time to relax."

Ethan still felt the need to make up for his behaviour at the hospital but in truth, he really wanted to see her again and this was the best excuse he could come up with to do so.

Smiling, Sophie was intrigued.

"Sure, why not?"

"I'll pick you up by one o'clock. See you then."

Hanging up the phone, Sophie contemplated her time with Ethan.

Interesting guy. Not sure why I've committed to doing something I have no idea what it is with someone I barely know but what the hell!

She certainly didn't completely understand it but she was actually very much looking forward to seeing Ethan again.

Arriving right on time, Sophie got into Ethan's car and couldn't wait to ask.

"So, where are you taking me? I'm dying to know."

"You're not a very patient person, are you?" He refused to give in. "You'll find out soon enough."

The drive wasn't more than thirty minutes before Ethan pulled up in front of a small airport.

"We're here."

Sophie followed Ethan into the building in front of them.

"But this is an airport. Why are we at an airport?" Sophie was confused and becoming anxious.

"You'll see."

Sophie waited while Ethan spoke to the person at the desk, filled out some paperwork, grabbed a folder, then signalled for her to follow him.

Walking out of the building through a gate and onto the tarmac, Sophie followed closely behind Ethan. It was quite windy out. Looking around she noticed people milling around the area, checking planes, boarding planes. There was a large fuel truck driving across the tarmac towards a row of planes at the far side of the airport. There were planes starting up, with one about to land. Sophie found it difficult to hear Ethan speaking to her as they went. Walking up to a small jet, she looked around for other passengers. Her eyes grew large as she watched Ethan walk around checking multiple outside areas of the plane before opening a hatch door and pulling steps down.

"This way."

Slowly climbing up the steps, she was trying to rein in her emotions. Walking into the plane she was distracted and hit her head on the top of the opening.

"Ow!"

"Oh...watch your head." Ethan grinned.

"Gee thanks!"

"This is a beautiful plane. Whose is it?" She was hoping this was just a short tour. With no intention of going further inside, Sophie anxiously stood near the exit ensuring a quick escape.

"It's a rental."

"Where's the pilot?" She was hoping there would be no pilot which would mean they weren't going flying.

"I'm the pilot."

"What?" She was confused. "Don't tell me you're going to fly this thing." Sophie uncomfortably joked.

"That's right."

"What?!" Panic started to set in.

"I'm going to fly this plane. I'm the pilot." Ethan nonchalantly responded as he began checking things in the plane. "Just give me a few minutes as I do my pre-flight check inside here and then we will be on our way. Oh, and you might want to sit up front. We won't be able to do much talking with you back here and besides, the view is much better from the cockpit."

Looking around she tentatively followed Ethan. Stepping into the cockpit, she was overwhelmed at the sight before her. It was a collection of buttons and switches with a whole lot of lights that Sophie had no clue about. Nervously sitting down, she was confused when Ethan pointed to the other seat.

"Not there. That's the pilot's seat. You can sit there."

"Beside you? There?"

"Yes. I'll be done in a few minutes and then we can head out." Ethan calmly continued with his pre-flight checks.

Sophie wasn't fond of flying in a big plane, let alone this small tin can and the thought of it wasn't helping the anxiety she was feeling. Sitting down, she was sure her nervousness was glaringly obvious. Looking around, her eyes opened wider. As Ethan continued with his preflight checks, Sophie looked behind her down the very short hallway to where she had been standing beforehand then turned to look out the cockpit window again.

"Are you sure this is safe?"

"Absolutely." Ethan answered, continuing with his checks.

Within a few minutes Ethan had finished, shut the hatch door, locked it, then sat down in the pilot's seat. Strapping himself in he looked at Sophie who was noticeably paler than she had been when he first picked her up.

"Are you feeling okay?"

"Yeah…yeah. I just don't fly…well…ever."

"You aren't nervous of flying are you?" Ethan began to realize what was going on.

Sophie considered her options. Lie and save face or be perfectly honest and look like a big chicken.

"I absolutely am nervous to fly." She waited for the judgement but none came. "I never fly because it terrifies me. That's why I take the train and in turn how I met your father, and hence how I met…"

"We don't have to…" Ethan interrupted.

"But I'm going to do it anyway." Cringing, she closed her eyes and scrunched up her nose. Biting down on her bottom lip she peeked through her narrowed eyes at Ethan. "Ahhh…I can't believe I just said that."

"Let me assure you, I'm a very qualified and experienced pilot. You are safe with me." Ethan grinned. "I've only ever crashed once."

"What?!"

"I'm kidding. I've never crashed." Ethan smiled as he reassured her.

Sophie felt a little self-conscious under Ethan's lingering gaze. Pushing her hair behind her ear she looked away.

"Ready to go?"

"What? Oh…sure. Let's do this before I change my mind."

"You won't regret it." Ethan reassured her.

I have my doubts. Sophie rolled her eyes.

FIFTEEN

Returning to the airport, Sophie stepped down the steps of the plane onto the tarmac.

"Ethan, that was absolutely spectacular! Where do I begin? The mountains, the ocean, it was all just so beautiful. I now have an appreciation for why you love to fly. You're in your own world up there! Really, it was indescribable!"

Sophie waited patiently while Ethan finished up with the plane and then walked with him to the terminal.

"I'm glad you enjoyed yourself." Ethan smiled.

"Thank you so much! I truly loved it! Admittedly, I had my doubts at first and well, as you know, I hate flying...well, I used to hate flying. Now I'm a changed woman. Although, I'm not so sure about a commercial flight, but this...this, I would do again. You really are a wonderful pilot. Those views! My God! Gorgeous! I've never seen the mountains look more beautiful than from a plane and well, the ocean...it gives you a whole new perspective doesn't it?"

"Sophie?"

"And you were absolutely correct. The view from the cockpit is the best. You can see just about everything from there..."

"Sophie?"

"...of course, I'm not saying it wasn't just a little bit terrifying taking off, but once you're up there it truly is a spectacle and I can't thank you enough for letting me fly the plane for a few minutes. That was an incredible..."

"Sophie!" Ethan had to speak loud enough to get her attention.

Surprised, Sophie stopped talking and looked at Ethan.

"Yes?"

"So, I assume you enjoyed yourself then?" Ethan grinned. "You certainly wear your heart on your sleeve."

Immediately feeling embarrassed, Sophie fidgeted with her necklace.

"I actually appreciate the emotion. It's a nice change from what I've been used to." Ethan was relieved to see Sophie break out into a big smile. "I'm glad you braved it out and came with me."

"I'm sorry. I tend to ramble when I'm excited."

"Please don't apologize. Rambling is fine."

"It really was wonderful, Ethan. Thank you." Sophie relaxed knowing that Ethan had not minded her excited chatter.

"Would you care to join me for dinner? Are you free?"

"I am free." Sophie wasn't sure what to make of this man. He seemed so private and put together and yet there was a side to him that was approachable and comfortable and really quite interesting.

"Your choice since you made such a good one the other night." Ethan waited.

"Well, I haven't been there in a number of years but there used to be a family pizzeria in the south-end of the city that was fabulous. Not sure if they are even still there. Bruno's I think?"

"Yes, Bruno's. I've heard of the place. I've never been a big pizza eater myself…"

"You'll never get better pizza than at Bruno's. Are you game?"

"Since you braved the flight, I think I can brave pizza."

"You won't regret it."

Ethan grinned. "Fair enough."

Sitting at a bistro table outside of Bruno's, a server carefully placed a very hot pepperoni pizza on the table between them. Picking up one of the plates, the waiter served a slice to Sophie then to Ethan. Picking up the bottle of red wine, the server popped the cork and poured a small amount of wine into one of the glasses for tasting. Sophie deferred to Ethan who sipped then nodded his approval and with that, the server poured them each a glass of wine then returned inside.

"You will love this pizza. It's wood oven baked and was always so delicious." Sophie picked up her slice and took a large bite. With her mouth still full, she said, "Oh my God! It's still just as good as I remember."

Watching Ethan pick up a knife and fork, Sophie had to stop him.

"No, no, no! What are you doing?"

"I'm going to cut my pizza."

"Oh no you're not! That's not how you eat pizza." She frowned. "You eat it with your hands."

Ethan immediately put the knife and fork down. "Really? Does it matter?"

"Yes, really, and it does matter." Sophie stood firm.

Looking down at the pizza, then back up at Sophie, Ethan picked up the slice and awkwardly aimed it towards his mouth before taking a large bite.

Sophie waited for the reaction.

"Admittedly, this is very good pizza." He finished eating the first bite then took a sip of wine.

"Have you never eaten pizza before?" Sophie teased as she shook her head.

"Of course I've eaten pizza before." Ethan defended. "Just because I eat it with a knife and fork shouldn't disqualify me as a pizza eater."

"I beg to differ." Sophie laughed.

"So, Ethan, tell me, why is a good looking guy like you not married?" She asked without even thinking.

Stopping eating, he just stared at her.

"You think I'm good looking?"

Sophie blushed with embarrassment.

"I...umm..."

"It's okay. I think I'm a pretty good-looking guy too." Ethan made light of her slip up. Continuing, he offered, "I have been married."

Sophie was relieved he let her off the hook so easily. Saying nothing, she allowed him to continue.

"It didn't work out."

"I'm sorry."

"It's okay; it was for the best." Pouring them each another glass of wine he asked, "And you? Why aren't you married?"

"Oh I don't know. Never met the right guy I suppose. My family... father...my father could be rather intimidating."

"Chased them all away, did he?" Ethan was happy to have the conversation revert back to Sophie.

"You could say that. More like my family was exhausting to be around."

"I see. Any siblings?"

"One sister and a brother-in-law, both obnoxious and self-absorbed. We aren't close. As a matter-of-fact, they aren't exactly happy with me right now."

"Do you like working for the family business?" Ethan was curious.

Thinking for a moment, Sophie wasn't sure how to respond.

"I do, but…" Hesitating she continued, "I don't know…since my parents died a couple of years ago the business has been more challenging."

"They died at the same time?" Ethan was sympathetic.

"Yes, they actually died together in a car crash. Bad weather and a tree didn't make their survival probable that night."

"Must have been difficult for you and your sister."

"Admittedly, it has been. I'm dealing with complications that were unforeseen and that's one of the reasons why I'm here. I have to deal with everything because, well…"

"The sense of responsibility weighs heavy."

"Yes, exactly." Sophie hesitated. "That, and the fact that my sister is creating more problems for me than she should."

Sitting quietly, the two sipped on wine and finished up the pizza. Sophie chuckled as she saw pizza sauce dripping down Ethan's chin onto his shirt.

"What? What are you laughing at?"

Signalling with her finger to his chin, Ethan frowned and wiped the sauce off his chin.

"And your shirt."

Ethan appeared annoyed as he wiped his shirt with the napkin, creating a stain larger than the spot itself.

"Hey relax, it's no biggie. So, you're a messy eater…" Sophie laughed.

Feeling a splash of water on her face, Sophie was taken aback. "Hey! What was that for?"

"Need I point out that if I had eaten with a knife and fork I wouldn't have dripped sauce on my shirt."

Sophie frowned as she saw Ethan laughing, then picked up her water glass.

"Don't you dare…I only splashed a little water on your face." Ethan stood up.

Sophie dared and threw the entire glass of water at Ethan, whose mouth dropped open, shocked that she would even consider such an atrocity.

"I can't believe you just did that. You're in trouble now."

"Hey you started it! You think I'm scared of you?" Sophie retorted.

"Oh, you should be. My motto is don't get mad, get even."

"I'll take my chances." Sophie was defiant.

"Okay then." And with that Ethan finished his wine, placed his glass back down then headed to the car.

Sophie's mouth dropped open. *Oh my God! He left me with the bill. Game on, Mr. Blackburn, game on.*

Paying the bill, Sophie caught up to Ethan who was standing leaning against his car, legs and arms crossed.

"Thanks for dinner." He grinned, then opened the passenger door for Sophie, before walking around and getting into the driver's seat.

Doing up her seatbelt, Sophie waited until he got in the car. "Can I offer you a napkin to dry off?"

"Don't try and make nice with me now. It's too late." Ethan smirked. "I'm not that easily swayed."

Sophie laughed. Looking over at Ethan, she was seeing a side of him she very much liked.

Starting the car, he offered, "I'll take you back to your hotel. I'm sure you will have seen quite enough of me by the end of the day tomorrow." Not that he was eager to take her back. He was thoroughly enjoying his time with her. He felt like he could actually relax with Sophie.

"Thank you." Sophie grinned. *A small part of her was disappointed.*

Arriving at the hotel, Sophie got out of the car and watched as he drove away. Waving good-bye, she was surprisingly disappointed he was leaving.

SIXTEEN

Saturday morning arrived and Sophie laid in bed a little longer than she should have, as she thought back to the day before. Ethan really had grown on her. There was something about him that she was drawn to…besides his yummy cologne.

Getting up and dressed, she quickly ran to the florist, then back to the hotel to get changed for her visit with Winston. She was looking forward to seeing him again. He'd seemed so sweet when she'd met him on the train.

Ethan had indicated he would pick her up at noon and she wanted to be ready when he arrived.

Fussing with her hair and make-up, she tried one outfit on after the other.

Finally deciding on a pair of chinos and a nice top and cardigan, Sophie slipped on a pair of flat shoes and gave herself one last look in the mirror. Frowning, she fussed with her hair once again and touched up her make-up.

"Perfume! I almost forgot perfume…and lipstick! Oh my God, what is wrong with me today?"

She was surprised to admit it but she was actually looking forward to seeing Ethan. He was just so interesting to be around, unlike so many other men she had met in recent years.

"Anyway, you're going to see Winston, not Ethan. Get yourself together, Sophie." Putting on her diamond heart shaped necklace, Sophie admired it in the mirror. It was a gift from her mother when she turned twenty-one and she wore it almost everyday. It had been handed down to Sophie's mother, by her mother, when she had turned twenty-one. One day it was expected that Sophie would hand it down to her own daughter when she turned of age. It was stunning but Sophie wasn't completely sure if she would ever have children, given her luck with men.

Grabbing her purse, the plants and wine, Sophie headed down to the lobby to wait for Ethan to arrive. It wasn't long before she saw him walking through the lobby.

"Ready to go?" He smiled. "Here, let me help you with those."

Sophie's heart fluttered ever so slightly, just enough to make her nervous. Taking in a breath, she was captivated once again by the smell of his cologne.

The man smells positively scrumptious. Get your shit together girl. The last thing you need is to fall for Ethan. Timing couldn't be less perfect.

As Ethan turned into a gated community, Sophie was surprised by the size of the homes which all seemed to be mini mansions in her opinion. She suspected Winston had money but she didn't expect this.

"Is this where your dad lives?" Sophie had to ask.

"Yes, but I moved in with him after my mother died."

"Oh, I see."

Pulling through automatic gates and onto a rather long driveway to the house, Sophie was in awe of how beautiful the property was.

This is a beautiful home."

"Thank you. A bit pretentious for my liking but it's not my home, so…"

Inviting Sophie into the house, they were greeted by a young woman who came out to the foyer. "Your father is in the library if you would like to join him there."

"Thank you, Paige. How is he feeling?"

"He's wonderful, all things considered. He's still trying to do too much so I have had to threaten him with no company at all unless he takes time to relax and be as calm as he can possibly be."

"Paige, this is Sophie, the woman who saved dad."

"A pleasure to meet you, Sophie. Thank you for your quick actions that saved Winston's life. What a wonderful thing you did."

"I just happened to be in the right place at the right time and did something anyone would have done, I'm sure." Sophie felt embarrassed by the accolades.

"Yes, well, you have not only Ethan's gratitude but mine as well."

Turning her attention to Ethan, Paige asked, "Is there anything I can do for you before I go to my suite?"

"Yes, please bring tea and pastries and I guess you had better bring some fruit as well."

"Yes, of course." Looking to Sophie, Paige added, "It's a pleasure to meet you."

Sophie smiled as she watched the young woman disappear down a hallway leading to seemingly the back of the house and the kitchen.

"Follow me." Ethan led the way.

Sophie walked down the long hall following quietly behind Ethan, admiring the beauty of Winston's home. She tried to discreetly peek into each of the rooms as they walked by them.

Office. Den? Living Room? Closed door. Wonder what that is?

There seemed to be more rooms than she could figure out what they were used for so she gave up trying.

"Dad, Sophie's here." Ethan announced as they walked into the library. Giving it a quick once over, Sophie acknowledged that it was most definitely a library with two out of four walls made up of bookcases filled with books. She always had loved the smell of books in any library or book store. She found the distinct aroma of the paper very appealing. She could spend hours in a book store wandering around, browsing through the books. It was always a place she could unwind. As a child she often begged her parents to let her go into any bookstore they happened upon. The memory made her smile.

Looking towards the sitting area, Sophie was thrilled to see Winston sitting there dressed much more casually than he had been when she met him on the train.

"Sophie, my dear! So wonderful to see you. Won't you please come and have a seat." Winston broke out into a wide smile upon seeing her.

"Please don't stand for me, Winston. It's not necessary." Walking over, she placed the pot of plants on the table in front of him. "These are for you." Leaning in, she gave him a big hug and a peck on the cheek.

"Not the wine?"

"Absolutely not! I don't want to get into trouble with your nurse…"

"Assistant."

"Your assistant then, or your son, for that matter. I've already experienced that nightmare." Sophie looked in Ethan's direction, raised her eyebrows and gave him a taunting smile.

Giving Sophie a blank stare, he mouthed, "Really?"

Sitting down in a rather large leather easy chair across from Winston, Sophie appreciated the warm fire roaring next to them. The day had turned rather chilly as far as she was concerned. It was October and they had been experiencing a much cooler season this year.

"I'll leave you both to catch up. If you'll excuse me." Ethan left the room, closing the doors behind him.

"So, how are you feeling, Winston?"

"I'm feeling wonderful, my dear. I couldn't be better other than Paige refuses to let me do business of any kind right now. Bit of a drill sergeant that one." Winston smiled warmly.

"And so you shouldn't be doing any work. Rest, relax and soon enough you will be back on your feet."

"Before we go any further, my dear, I must express to you my deepest gratitude for saving my life. I wouldn't be here today complaining about not being able to work had it not been for you."

Sophie was embarrassed by his sincere words.

"Winston...I..."

"And I must apologize for my son's abysmal behaviour at the hospital. He completely over reacted and I was extremely disappointed in him."

"Winston, really, it's okay."

"No, it really isn't. My dear, our paths crossed at a most opportune moment and I will forever be in your debt."

"I only did what anyone else would have done. I just happened to be in the right place at the right time. But admittedly, you did give me quite a scare."

"Sophie, please, I wouldn't be here today if it weren't for your quick actions. From what I understand you remained calm, you clearly knew what to do. I'm alive as a result. It was all very commendable and that's an understatement in my humble opinion." Looking at the young lady sitting in front of him, Winston could tell she was uncomfortable, but added, "I would like to do something for you…"

"No! Absolutely not! Everything you've said has been humbling. Inviting me for dinner is thanks enough as far as I'm concerned."

Just then the double doors opened.

Sophie looked to see the same young woman from the front door, entering the room with a tray carrying refreshments as Ethan had requested.

"Ah, thank you, Paige."

"Here you go." Placing the tray down on the table that sat between Winston and Sophie, she stood back up and addressed Winston.

"Will that be all?"

"Yes, thank you, Paige."

"Very well, I'll be in my suite should you need me, otherwise, I'll be back to check on you within the hour."

"Make it two." Winston insisted.

"But…"

"Make it two, Paige." Winston was firm on the matter.

"Yes, of course." And with that Paige exited the room closing the doors behind her.

"Let me pour that for you." Sophie reached for the pot and poured them each what she thought would be coffee.

"Damn that woman! She knows I wanted coffee." Winston frowned.

Smelling the hot liquid, Sophie smiled, "Ah but she knows very well that green tea is much better for you."

"And where are my pastries? She knows I have pastries every afternoon. I can assure you that I don't want blasted fruit. I'm not sure what I pay her for."

"I believe you pay her for exactly what she is doing. Now stop complaining." Sophie was stern but grinned in his direction unphased by his frustration. "Seems to me you are just a tad on the grouchy side this afternoon."

Sighing, Winston picked up the tea. Smelling it, he scrunched up his nose before putting it back down again.

"Yes, well..."

"Well, nothing. You must take care of yourself. I didn't save your damn life to have you drinking and eating things that are unhealthy for you. Now drink up and eat some of that lovely fruit." Sophie filled a small plate with said fruit and handed it to Winston who very reluctantly accepted it.

"Admittedly, Paige is a wonderful personal assistant. She's been with me for ten years now and I suppose I've given her much leeway but there are days she infuriates me."

"No doubt, some days, the feeling is likely mutual."

Looking up at Sophie, Winston squinted his eyes and very sternly stared her down. Sophie refused to flinch.

"You're not as agreeable as you came across on the train," he teased.

"Nor are you." Sophie winked in his direction as she fidgeted with her necklace.

"Hmphf." Winston frowned.

"That's a lovely necklace you have there."

Realizing she had been fussing with it, Sophie let it go.

"Thank you."

"Where did you get it? It's very unusual."

"My mother actually gave it to me when I turned twenty-one and her mother had given it to her."

"Really? I've only ever seen one similar but that was a long time ago. It's lovely." Winston stared at the necklace a moment longer before carrying on.

"So, I understand my son took you to dinner the other night. The least he could do given his behaviour towards you at the hospital."

"It was a misunderstanding and yes, he took me to dinner. I understand it's a place you had frequented when he was younger, Larry's Lobster Shack."

"My goodness, yes! I knew Larry very well back in the day. We were business acquaintances. I do believe he has retired and his son is running the place now. I'm surprised Ethan suggested you go there. Rather unlike my son as he much prefers fine dining establishments."

"It was my suggestion actually." Sophie smiled. "But, he was all for it, and it was quite delicious. I hadn't had lobster in a very long time so I was happy to have some, not to mention, the wonderful bottle of wine that Ethan brought along."

"Now that makes much more sense." Winston laughed. "As long as he made amends…"

"Yes, of course he did. We had a lovely evening. We even went to the beach and had a fire."

Winston's eyebrows immediately raised. "Is that so?" He grinned. "Lobster, a bottle of wine *and* a beach fire."

"Oh yes, I can't remember the name of the wine but he said it was a favourite of his."

"I know the one. A California red, if I recall. So, my son had lobster, his favourite bottle of wine then sat on a beach having a fire?" Winston wanted to clarify.

"Well, yes." Sophie seemed confused by Winston's reaction.

"Interesting."

"Is there something wrong?" Sophie was getting the sense that Winston didn't approve.

"No, not at all, my dear. Did you enjoy yourself?" Winston warmly smiled reassuring Sophie that all was well.

"I really did."

"Did Ethan explain the history behind his reaction towards you at the hospital?"

"No, he didn't." Sophie grew quite interested in what Winston was about to say.

"Well, it mainly stems from not long after my wife died. I met a very beautiful woman who was much younger than I was. We dated and spent much time together. Admittedly, I found her to be very charming but unfortunately, she wasn't in the relationship to be with me so much as she was in the relationship for my money. She started asking me for help financially. It started off in small amounts, car repairs here, house repairs there…then it worked its way up to credit card debt, her car completely breaking down and claimed she had no money to purchase a new one. Well, you can imagine how it escalated over time. Suffice to say, that once Ethan realized what was going on he very sternly sent her on her way and proceeded to scold me for being so naive."

"That's terrible! How can anyone be so shallow or unscrupulous?" Sophie was shocked.

"They are out there, Sophie. I am not generally a naive person, however, she was very charming and I was very captivated. It's sad when you're an old man, lonely after the loss of your wife then to receive companionship from such a woman." Sophie felt bad for Winston who was looking quite sad at the moment. "Well, I learned my lesson."

"I think it's despicable behaviour and I'm glad to hear Ethan stepped in."

"Yes…well…now he's very cautious with the people he lets into our lives." Nodding his head slightly. "He's a little too suspicious if you want my opinion. You have to trust people at some point, you can't go through life with such a jaded outlook. I can tell you I've had more experience with kind, sincere individuals than I have those with ill intent."

"I can certainly understand his over-reaction with me given what you experienced." Sophie suddenly felt sad for both men.

The afternoon went by quickly as Sophie and Winston talked about travel, trains, and family. The conversation was easy and enjoyable. Sophie was grateful she'd agreed to come. She'd found Winston to be a very interesting man. She couldn't help but acknowledge yet again how much he reminded her of her father. He seemed to be kind, fair and quite a dedicated family man.

Although, that's where Winston and Daddy differ. Daddy wasn't as dedicated to his family as she had thought. He was quite caught up in his work… too caught up at times. He was rarely home, meetings day and night. There wasn't a lot of time for Mom or us girls when we were older but there was never any doubt that he loved us.

Her thoughts were suddenly interrupted by Ethan's return.

"Are you both getting caught up on things?"

"Why yes, as a matter of fact, we are. I'm hearing all about your lobster dinner." Winston grinned. "You remember, Ethan, the one with the beach fire and your favourite bottle of wine."

Ethan ignored his father's innuendo.

"Sophie, I certainly hope my father is keeping you entertained and not boring you with tales of the past."

Looking over at Winston, Sophie thought how tired he was looking.

"Absolutely and yes, he did share some tales of the past and I found them very interesting."

"See son, not everyone finds my stories boring." Winston grinned in his son's direction with a look of touché on his face.

Just then, as promised, Paige arrived back at the library announcing that it was time for Winston to have a nap.

"I'm not a child, Paige. I don't need a nap." Winston retorted.

"Well, you're acting like one. Now let's go. If you don't follow doctor's orders then there will be no more company for you. I already left you much longer than I should have." Paige was kind but firm. "I'll not argue with you."

"I would do as you're told, Winston. I think Paige has the upper hand right now."

Paige acknowledged her appreciation with a nod towards Sophie.

"Now, don't you be siding with her, Sophie. She's a drill sergeant and requires no encouragement from you." Winston stood up. "I'll see you both at dinner."

"I'm looking forward to it." Sophie walked over and gave Winston a hug. "Behave yourself. I want to be allowed to come back and visit you," she whispered in his ear.

Watching them leave the room and shutting the doors behind them, Sophie scanned the room.

"He is a stubborn old bear." Ethan grinned.

"Well, he was looking rather tired. I shouldn't have kept him so long." Sophie glanced over at a set of books. Wandering over to take a closer look, she was impressed by the collection of old classics. "This is a wonderful collection of books. Do you read?" Sophie was curious.

"Yes, my mother instilled that in me at a very young age. She was an avid reader." Ethan walked over, standing beside Sophie admiring the collection. "I loved the old classics. Shakespeare...on the other hand...I never had the slightest interest in."

"Me either. I just could never understand it enough to enjoy it." Walking along, Sophie was surprised to see a set of books with a familiar name on them. "Your father writes?"

Walking over, Ethan shook his head. "No actually, I write."

"But..."

"Yes, my first name is Winston."

"Really? So, you are Winston Ethan Blackburn?"

"Indeed I am. Named after my father and my mother's brother."

"Do you do much writing and are they always about hotels?" Looking at the covers, she asked, "And specifically historic hotels?"

"Well, I did at the time. I haven't written much in awhile..." Ethan added, "I was actually a history major at university." Ethan cleared his throat. "Listen, would you like to take a walk around the grounds?"

"That would be nice." Sophie wanted to continue with their conversation but clearly Ethan didn't.

"Follow me." It was more of a request than an order but Sophie jumped to attention the moment Ethan spoke the words.

SEVENTEEN

"My God, Ethan, it's so beautiful here."

"I suppose it is, yes." Ethan seemed indifferent.

"Do you ever just look around you and see the beauty here?"

Looking around them, Ethan answered, "I did at one time, yes, but I guess I've been much too busy in recent years, and especially recently, to pay much attention anymore."

"Well, you should because it's gorgeous."

Turning a corner, Sophie's mouth dropped open.

"You have tennis courts? As if the pool wasn't enough and this spectacular home?"

Sophie was in awe. They had grown up with money but her father always had them live rather modestly. Sophie hadn't known the difference growing up, but as an adult she realized just how modest her family's lifestyle was in comparison to those in similar financial circles. It was just who they were. They never liked to flaunt their wealth and much preferred to keep things low-key.

Standing looking at the tennis courts, Sophie asked, "Do you play?"

"I do."

"Shall we?"

"Excuse me?" Ethan was surprised by the request.

"Shall we play?"

"Well…"

"Are you afraid I'll beat you?" Sophie was confident in her ability. She had grown up playing tennis and had competed for a number of years in her teens. She relished the challenge. "Because I can," she taunted.

"I wouldn't be so confident."

"Oh, but I am." She was intentionally baiting him.

"How do you know I'm not a pro?"

"I don't."

"Do you think I can't beat you?" Ethan challenged.

"I definitely think *I* can beat *you*." Sophie was steadfast.

"Really?" Ethan stared her down without a flicker of emotion.

"Yeah, really." Sophie reciprocated.

Ethan grew momentarily quiet. "Follow me. You can't play in those shoes. We have extra shoes in the tennis hut."

Sophie quickly stepped in line with his pace and in no time at all they were on the courts.

Sophie asked, "Do you want up or down?"

"Up."

Sophie spun her racket and Ethan won.

"I choose to serve."

Ethan prepared to serve.

Sophie found herself battling it out with Ethan as he quickly took the lead.

"Fifteen Love." Ethan stated a little too confidently as far as Sophie was concerned. Fighting back hard, she quickly tied the game.

"Fifteen All."

Continuing with their game, Ethan became annoyed when Sophie took the lead.

"Fifteen Thirty."

Sophie was impressed with his skills. He was good.

"Thirty All." Ethan smirked.

Well, well, well, the man can play.

She hadn't played tennis in a long time and now regretted boasting about her skills. Her confidence of beating him was waning ever so slightly. Sophie was growing more determined to win this match. Wiping the sweat from her forehead, Sophie stood ready for the serve. There was a long rally. Sophie finished it off with an overhead smash.

"Thirty Forty,"

Sophie readied herself.

Ethan was very pleased to ace Sophie.

"Deuce." He shouted with confidence.

Ethan served once again but Sophie returned with a winner.

"Ad Out."

"Take that old man!" Sophie was rather pleased with herself.

"Old man?"

Looking up, she grinned, seeing the look on Ethan's face.

"Yup. I call it as I see it."

Frustrated, Ethan marched up to the service line again and fired another ace.

"Deuce," he yelled.

The sound of the ball hitting the rackets back and forth was all that could be heard besides their grunts as they swung and hit.

With some great shots, Sophie won the next two points and took the first game.

They continued to battle it out and before they realized it they had played for almost two hours and Sophie had squeaked out a win, winning two out of three sets.

"Match over!" Sophie gratefully shouted. "Oh, thank God." She momentarily bent over resting both hands on her knees. She was exhausted.

Walking up to the net they shook hands.

"Well done." Sophie was completely out of breath and wiped the sweat off her forehead. "This was tough. I haven't played in quite a long time."

"It shows." Ethan teased.

"Very funny." Her sarcasm was intentional.

Ignoring her, Ethan offered, "You played well. You're a worthy opponent."

"Well, thank you. As were you." Sophie walked with him to put the rackets and balls back into the shed and change her shoes.

"I'll show you where you can go to freshen up before dinner."

EIGHTEEN

Dinner was soon being served and Sophie couldn't help but think how incredible the dining room was as she walked into the room. Large oil paintings everywhere, a glorious chandelier, a table that could sit a dozen or more people, the magnificent carpet…Persian, she speculated.

Being escorted to her seat by someone she assumed was the server, Sophie looked down to see multiple forks, spoons, glasses. She began to feel slightly uncomfortable. This was far more than she had expected or was used to. Ethan was seated across the table from her and it wasn't long before Winston walked in and was seated at the end of the table between them.

"So, what did the two of you do while I forcibly took a nap." Winston thanked the server as a napkin was placed in his lap.

"I took Sophie for a walk around the grounds." Ethan didn't elaborate.

"Very good and Sophie I hope you enjoyed your tour."

"Very much so, Winston. As a matter of fact we played tennis afterwards." Sophie was thrilled to have played on such impeccable courts.

Ethan quickly shook his head, no, in Sophie's direction.

Looking at Sophie with raised eyebrows, Winston immediately looked in Ethan's direction. "Really?"

Sighing, Ethan squirmed under his father's stare, then quickly changed the subject. "So what is for dinner tonight, Thomas?"

Thomas, who Sophie assumed was the server, immediately answered.

"Prime rib, sir." Thomas began to pour the wine Sophie brought, as he spoke.

Sophie observed Thomas, who appeared to be roughly in his fifties, with a well groomed moustache, dark hair with grey sides. He was tall, she guessed perhaps six feet give or take, slim, and someone with a very friendly face.

Winston's stare lingered on his son before turning to speak to their guest.

"I hope you're hungry, Sophie."

"Yes, I certainly am after that tennis match."

Sophie noticed the subtlety of Winston's looks in his son's direction and wondered what was going on. She questioned if perhaps she was an intrusion into their private lives. Something they weren't completely comfortable with, given the past.

"Who won?" Winston asked with great interest.

"I did." Sophie responded, "But, for an old man he played rather well," she teased.

"Is that right?" Winston chuckled. "Interesting."

Sophie suddenly felt uncomfortable. She sensed Winston's disapproval. *Perhaps I'm crossing the line and they are just being polite. Maybe I shouldn't have asked to play tennis.*

"I'm sorry, did I overstep asking to play?"

"Not at all, my dear, that's what those courts are for. Certainly not someone like me who can barely get around these days. I'm quite impressed with your tennis skills. Ethan hasn't lost a match in a very long time. He used to play competitively in his university days and was a hard one to beat." Winston boasted.

Squinting her eyes, Sophie stared across at Ethan.

"Is that so?" She was now skeptical that he had given it his all, although she knew she had played very well. "You had better have tried your best out there."

Winston replied before Ethan had a chance to speak.

"Oh, Sophie, that is not Ethan's style. He most certainly would have tried his best. He's very competitive. There is no doubt that you won fair and square." Winston reassured her. "Which is precisely why I am surprised. He must be out of shape."

"Okay good, because otherwise I would have had to challenge you to another match and it wouldn't have been pretty."

"I've no doubt." Ethan nodded in her direction.

Seeing a flicker of humour in Ethan's eyes, Sophie felt comfortable that it had not been a 'charity' game.

Winston glanced from Sophie to Ethan and back again. Grinning, he said nothing.

Within moments, Sophie was thanking Thomas as he placed her dinner in front of her. It looked delicious. The room was full of the savoury smell of prime rib, Yorkshire pudding and gravy. Her mouth was watering as the aroma wafted through the room. She had to admit she was suddenly very hungry.

After dinner, they moved back to the library where a fire was roaring. The smell of the wood burning immediately resonated with Sophie. There was no smell that instantaneously relaxed her more than that of a wood burning fire. It was a smell that took her back to the summer days of her teens, sitting around a campfire with her friends, singing, lots of laughter and getting seriously drunk.

"A liqueur, Sophie?" Winston offered.

"Yes, that would be lovely, thank you."

Looking in his son's direction, Ethan immediately walked over and poured himself and Sophie a liqueur. Pouring his father some tea, he passed it along to the sound of Winston quietly moaning over the fact that it was green tea again.

Within moments, Thomas arrived and placed a tray of pastries and fruit on the table.

"Will there be anything else, sir?"

"No, thank you, Thomas." Winston smiled at the other gentleman.

Leaving the room, Thomas shut the doors behind him.

"I trust you enjoyed dinner." Winston watched as Sophie sat in one of the easy chairs in front of the fireplace.

"It was fabulous. Thank you again. It was not necessary but very much appreciated."

"I hope you will come back and visit again soon."

"I would love to."

"Do you know yet how long you will be in town?" Ethan asked. Winston took great interest in the fact that Ethan was even asking.

"I'm not sure. As I mentioned to you the other night, I have some family business to attend to and then, quite honestly, I'm not even sure what I'll do after that. There is a lot to consider."

Sophie didn't even want to think about it at all. The future was unknown at the moment. Just the thought of what may lie ahead created a great deal of anxiety in her.

"If there is anything we can help you with, Sophie, please ask. Ethan and I would be more than happy to assist."

"Thank you, Winston. I will keep that in mind." Sophie appreciated the offer but knew this was nothing with which anyone could help her.

"What line of work are you in, Sophie? I don't think you mentioned what you do." Winston was curious to learn more of his young guest.

"It's a family business. One my parents started up when they were in their twenties as a matter of fact." Sophie wasn't ready to get into it with them. She too was cautious about discussing too much about the family business especially given the current circumstances. "How about yourself, Winston?"

"Our business too is family run. I originally started it up with two business partners who eventually went their own way and now that Ethan has stepped in to help me, he has managed to modernize things. Something that was required if we wanted to remain relevant."

"Oh really? Wonderful!" Sophie smiled in Ethan's direction who was looking rather uncomfortable with the accolades.

"We own a chain of hotels." Winston stated.

Sophie's mouth dropped open and her heart skipped a beat. Her palms became sweaty and she failed to notice that she was holding her breath. *Oh my God! It couldn't be.* She was starting to put two and two together.

"The Tuxedo chain." Winston added.

Are you kidding me? How could I have not realized this? The name, Blackburn, of course. Callaghan Hotels biggest competitor.

"Really?" Sophie was having a difficult time knowing how to respond. "You mean you own the Tuxedo Marquis and the Tuxedo Chateau hotels in Montreal?"

"Yes, that's right."

"And the Tuxedo Tower here in town?"

"Amongst others across the country, yes." Winston smiled. "You are familiar with them?"

"Yes, definitely."

"Had you not already had accommodation at the C-Granite we would have put you up at the Tuxedo Tower during your stay here. After all, you did save my life and I would have been more than pleased to do so." Winston smiled.

Biting down on her lip, she grew extremely uncomfortable. Her mind was racing.

"Oh, yes, thank you, that would have been lovely."

Dammit! How could I have been so distracted to not even realize the connection? Oh boy, this definitely complicates things.

"You know...I really must be going. I have an early day tomorrow..."

Winston looked slightly taken aback, but said nothing. Looking over to Ethan who immediately stood up, he said, "Of course. Ethan will take you back to your hotel."

"I can take an Uber, it's quite alright."

"I wouldn't hear of it. No, Ethan will take you."

"Yes, I'll take you, Sophie. It's no trouble."

Standing up, Sophie walked over to Winston.

"Thank you for a lovely visit, Winston. I'm sorry I have to cut our evening short."

"Come again soon, my dear." Winston smiled warmly.

"Sure...yes..." Sophie wasn't sure whether she should say something or keep quiet. She decided on the latter.

Leaning in to give Winston a hug and kiss on the cheek, she said, "You take care and do as you're told." Quickly grabbing her coat and purse, she followed Ethan out of the room and to the car.

Sophie remained quiet during the drive home. Her mind was spinning with what Winston had divulged.

"Did something upset you?" Ethan broke the uncomfortable silence.

"Pardon?" Sophie had been deep in thought.

"You seem upset about something. Did dad say something to offend you?"

"Oh, no. Not at all. I was getting tired and I do have an early day tomorrow."

"Okay, as long as you're sure."

"Absolutely. Everything's fine." Sophie was having a hard time sounding convincing.

"Would you be interested in joining my father and I for dinner again next week? He really did enjoy your visit." Ethan didn't want to divulge just how much he had been enjoying Sophie's company since he met her.

Sophie grew very uncomfortable. The whole scenario bothered her. She had been enjoying her time with both Winston and Ethan and now this would ruin any possibility of that again.

"I...umm...I really don't think so. I mean...I'm busy with...family stuff." Sophie stumbled with her words.

"Of course, perhaps one evening the following week then." Ethan offered.

"Perhaps. I'll have to get back to you about that."

Pulling up in front of the hotel, Sophie quickly got out of the car.

Saying good-bye to Ethan before he could say another word, Sophie shut the car door and stood watching as he drove away. Standing in front of the hotel, she was unable to think straight.

How the hell do I get myself into these situations? What are the chances? Thank God I never gave them my last name.

"Ms Callaghan, I'll get the door for you."

Turning to see the door being held open, Sophie turned to head inside.

"Thank you, Steve."

Once in her suite, Sophie flopped down on the bed. She suddenly felt very exhausted.

Could things get any more complicated than they already are? As if I don't have enough on my mind, this just makes things even worse. The last thing I need them to find out is that my family owns the Callaghan C-line of hotels, their biggest competitor in the business. My God, Ethan would really think I was out for money, or worse, inside information from his father.

NINETEEN

MONDAY MORNING, SOPHIE DECIDED THAT today was the day to make the phone call she so dreaded. She hadn't slept well since having dinner with Winston and Ethan. There was too much on her mind. She needed to deal with her mother's estate or lose her sanity. That whole situation with Winston and Ethan was just one complication too many, one that she couldn't deal with at the moment. She would deal with this other matter then leave town. They wouldn't be any the wiser.

Standing staring out her very quiet room window, she looked below to see cars driving by, pedestrians rushing along, fire trucks and police sirens blaring as their lights flashed frantically to their next call. The sun was shining, leaves were turning colour. Life just managed to carry on while hers seemed to be at a standstill. Sighing, she picked up the phone and dialled the lawyer's office.

"Good morning. Maison, McIlroy and Hawthorne, how may I help you?"

The same male voice, as previously, answered the phone. Sophie couldn't speak at first.

"Hello?" The male voice echoed in her ear.

Clearing her throat, Sophie finally found her nerve.

"Yes, hello."

"How may I help you?" The young man sounded less interested in helping than he did about getting to the next call.

"Yes, I'm looking for Mr. Hawthorne please."

"May I tell him who is calling?"

"My name is Sophie Callaghan. I was asked to contact Mr. Hawthorne about a family matter by Mr. Morganstern of Morganstern, Stone and Turelly in Cedardale.

"I'm aware of the law firm. One moment."

Alrighty then. Rather curt for the first voice of a law firm.

"Mr. Hawthorne will be with you in a moment. Please hold."

It wasn't long before Mr. Hawthorne answered the line.

"Ms Callaghan, Marcel Hawthorne here. I was of the understanding that Mr. Morganstern was taking care of business regarding your mother's estate."

"That is correct...well, it was correct, however, he hadn't heard from you in months and I offered to come down and deal with things in person. Given the circumstances, I am more than interested in the outcome, as you can well imagine." Sophie was no longer nervous and her business demeanor took over.

"Ah yes, well, Mr. Morganstern hasn't heard from me because I haven't heard from my client with anything definitive. I had spoken to my client several months ago when I explained the situation. At that time, they said they couldn't talk and they would get back to me. I have had my office follow up multiple times. Each time there was a reason why they couldn't respond back to me. It has now been a week since I last contacted my client and at that time I was notified that they have not yet been able to pursue the matter further."

"And when does your client expect to pursue this and what's to pursue? We have three weeks to get these papers signed. It's been months."

Sophie was annoyed. "We really don't want this to drag on. As you can imagine, my family is wanting to get the legalities sorted out so we know how to move forward. Why does this need to go through this family member first?"

"Apparently, your mother stated within the letter that was forwarded to us that their family member needs to deal with the matter initially, therefore, that is who we are waiting on."

"It's so frustrating though. I don't understand why mother set things up this way."

"I understand your frustration, Ms Callaghan. That said, it has become somewhat more complicated."

"Why is that?"

"There was a death in the family. On top of that I was just notified that there has been a personal emergency my client has had to deal with. There is not much that I can do to push this along, Ms Callaghan."

"Well, you must. We have very limited time and it is in everyone's best interest to wrap this matter up as quickly as possible. I sympathize with your client's personal situation, however, they have had plenty of time to deal with this matter and now it is just becoming problematic for all parties involved." Sophie was incensed.

"I will contact my client again and express the urgency of the situation."

"I would appreciate that, Mr. Hawthorne. If it would help expedite the situation, I would be happy to meet with your client to discuss this further."

She knew that was complete and utter bullshit. She had no interest in meeting this person face to face. The thought terrified her but she knew, eventually, it would have to happen.

"I'm sure that will be unnecessary, Ms Callaghan, but I will pass that along to my client. Once I have some definitive answers, I will contact you."

"Preferably by the end of the week, Mr. Hawthorne."

"I will do my best."

Giving him her mobile number, Sophie thanked Mr. Hawthorne then hung up.

What the hell is going on with this client of his? I feel terrible that there was a death in the family but it makes no sense that they haven't taken time out to deal with this, whatever it is they need to deal with.

Sophie was completely agitated.

Picking up the phone once again, Sophie called Mr. Morganstern and updated him on the current situation.

"Is there nothing that can be done?"

"I'm sorry, Sophie, they legally have until the end of the month."

"I understand that, but this has been going on for months."

"Yes, but our most recent communication gave them until the end of October so we must be patient and wait."

Mr. Morganstern was an older gentleman, very patient, very compassionate. Sophie adored him. He had been her mother's lawyer for decades and she trusted him.

"Okay, but should I wait here until the end of the month or should I just come home?"

"That's entirely up to you. There is a little less than three weeks to go. If you have some other business in Granite Hill then stay, otherwise, I would suggest coming home and getting on with things until we hear back from them."

"Thank you Mr. Morganstern. I appreciate what you're doing. I'm just a bit impatient, I suppose." Sophie knew how hypocritical she was being. She had, in fact, been reluctant to deal with this but now that the ball was rolling she wanted to get it wrapped up. She wasn't sure what the outcome would be – no one really knew.

Sitting in her suite, Sophie was trying to clear her head and decide whether to stay or go. She decided to wait until the end of the week and if there was no word, she would head home and let the lawyers deal with things.

Hearing her phone ring, she looked to see who was calling.

"Damn. I cannot speak to Ethan today or this week for that matter." Ignoring the call she showered. Hearing the phone ring once again, she hoped it wasn't Ethan calling back. Getting dressed, she put some make-up on and checked her phone. Seeing that Tony had called, she made a mental note to call him later on.

Riding down the elevator to go out and do some shopping, her phone rang once again. Seeing that it was Ethan, she thought she would answer it and make up some excuse not to talk long.

"Oh hi, Ethan."

"Hi Sophie. I was wondering if you were free for a coffee?"

Sophie debated lying or not. *I'm doing that far too often lately.* She hated to lie. They had been so kind to her.

"Unfortunately, I'm not well today, Ethan. I'm in bed fighting a bit of a bug." As the elevator reached the lobby floor, the door opened and Sophie stepped out. "I'm sorry. Perhaps another day. I think I'll just stay in bed today."

"I'm sorry to hear that."

"Yes, I'm just feeling the worst and decided to stay in my pajamas and rest up." Sophie never was a good liar but felt she was actually believable. "I'm feeling exhausted."

"Yes, I can see that." Ethan replied.

What? What does he mean by that?

"Pardon me?" Sophie had reached the lobby when she saw Ethan stand up, phone to his ear, looking at her with disbelieving eyes.

Dropping her arm holding the phone to her side, Sophie stopped walking and hung her head. Hanging up the phone, she placed it into her purse.

"Sick? Bed?" Ethan was not amused.

"Look, Ethan…"

"You don't owe me an explanation, Sophie. I'm sorry to have bothered you."

Turning to leave, Sophie called out to him but he ignored her.

"Ethan, please."

"It's fine, Sophie. I don't know what's going on here but that's fine. I just thought you were someone who didn't hide behind lies. You surprise me, that's all."

"Ethan!"

Watching as he walked out of the hotel, Sophie felt ashamed. Grabbing her phone, she tried to call him but naturally he didn't answer.

"Ethan, please call me back. I'm sorry. That was completely uncalled for."

She tried all morning to get a hold of him with no luck. He clearly was refusing to answer her calls.

"Ethan, let me explain. Please call me back."

When he still didn't call her back, she gave up. She deserved to be given the cold shoulder. What she did was wrong and she really wasn't sure how she would make it up to him anyway. She was afraid to tell him the truth. What would they…he…think of her?

The next day, Sophie tried once again to call Ethan. This time she decided she would come clean with why she was trying to avoid him. The truth always was best and quite frankly she was a lousy liar.

"Ethan, could we please talk? I was wrong and I'm sorry but if we could just meet I'll explain why…anyway, please call me. I'll even pay for dinner…your choice this time." She would try her best at manipulation to see if that would render results.

When he didn't answer her last call she gave up trying. He was clearly angry and she couldn't blame him. She deserved to be ignored.

She decided to start packing up to go home. She was tired and would let the lawyers deal with everything moving forward. She felt her welcome in Granite Hill had been overstayed, especially given the circumstances with Ethan.

Pulling out her suitcase, she jumped when her phone rang. Looking at it she was relieved to see it was him.

"Ethan?"

"I choose Frigo's. I'll see you there tonight at seven o'clock. Be prepared to explain yourself and you are definitely paying the check." And with that he hung up the phone.

Sophie wasn't sure whether to be very afraid or excited at the prospect of meeting up with him. She decided to go with excited and a heavy dose of very afraid along with it.

Damn! He knows very well I have nothing fancy to wear and now I'll have to go shopping.

TWENTY

Pulling up in front of Frigo's, Sophie looked out the taxi window before the valet opened the door, allowing her to step out. Leaning in to pay, she stood back up and was immediately greeted by the valet who opened the restaurant door, nodding as she walked past.

Walking inside, Sophie was impressed by the elegance of Frigo's. Looking around, she was taken by how contemporary it was. There was a back accent wall of rustic brick, dark wood flooring with pendant lights glowing softly over each table. Looking to her left, Sophie was impressed by the wall that substituted for a glass wine display exhibiting dozens of various wines, seemingly for even the most discerning of tastes. Looking around she noticed a dimly lit lounge to her right with a fireplace warmly illuminating the area. Looking around the restaurant Sophie couldn't see Ethan and patiently waited for the maître d' to approach her. "Would you be Sophie?"

Surprised that he knew her name, she nodded. "Yes."

"Follow me."

Walking through the intimate restaurant, Sophie could hear classical music quietly playing and the muffled voices of patrons talking. Looking around, Sophie admired the charm it offered. Every table was set with a white linen table cloth, upholstered chairs of light grey, crystal wine and water glasses, shiny cutlery, glass vases with roses and greenery in each and a candle flickering in the dimmed light. The sound of cutlery clinking on plates even had a distinguished sound to it. The mouth-watering aroma of seared steak and garlic wafted throughout. Servers were quietly delivering baskets of bread and butter, pouring water or wine for their assigned tables. One server was lighting what appeared to be cherries jubilee and allowing the flames to die down before carefully pouring it over the ice cream in front of guests whose faces lit up with delight at the spectacle.

The maître d' led Sophie to a far corner of the restaurant, which was somewhat private yet still allowed one to enjoy the rest of the beautiful restaurant setting. Sitting at the table was Ethan, who stood as she approached.

"I'll take your coat, Miss."

Handing the maître d' her coat, he carefully placed it over his one arm.

"After you." He pulled out her chair and gently pushed it back in as Sophie sat down.

"Your server will be with you momentarily."

Sophie watched as he turned and left. Turning back to look at Ethan across the table from her, she nervously fussed with her hair which she had pulled up into a loose bun. Carefully hanging her purse over the upholstered chair back, she felt extremely uncomfortable after her behaviour.

"You clean up nicely," he teased. In all honesty, he thought she looked absolutely stunning.

"Yes…well…I had no choice but to go shopping because you may not have remembered that I didn't have anything dressy to wear."

"Oh, I remembered," he grinned.

Nodding, Sophie quietly acknowledged the reasoning behind the sentiment. "Fair enough."

"I figured the classic little black dress and strappy heels would work here."

"It does." Ethan agreed. "Your shopping paid off. You look beautiful." The look on Ethan's face reassured Sophie that he was sincere.

Blushing, she felt self-conscious. She hadn't dressed up like this in a very long time. It was flattering to know it was appreciated.

"Thank you."

"Wine?" Ethan picked up the bottle of red off the table. "I told our server I would take care of pouring."

"Yes, thank you."

Filling their glasses, Ethan placed the bottle back onto the table.

"Cheers." He held his glass up to Sophie.

Picking hers up, she tapped the side of his glass which tinged as she did so.

"Cheers." Thinking for a moment she added, "To forgiveness."

Ethan grinned and quietly nodded, "To forgiveness."

Taking a sip, she placed the glass back down, now grateful she hadn't driven as she had originally planned.

"Ethan, I would like to apologize to you and explain…"

At that moment, their server walked up, poured water and left again.

Sighing, Sophie wasn't sure where to begin.

What the hell is wrong with me? I've never felt as discombobulated in my life as I have since meeting Ethan. Why is this all so difficult? I suppose if I just told him everything I could finally relax but then he might think I've been trying to take advantage of his father. How much do I divulge?

"You started to say something?" Ethan sat back and waited.

"Yes…well, I wanted to apologize." Sophie felt completely ill-at-ease. "You know…for lying to you."

Ethan's gaze was intense adding to Sophie's discomfort.

"It was wrong…"

Ethan remained silent as Sophie continued.

"It was wrong and I would like to explain why…"

Once again the server arrived at their table.

"Would you like to order an appetizer?" He looked at Ethan who in turn looked over at Sophie.

"Sophie?"

"No, thank you. I really don't have much of an appetite."

"Are you sure? They have wonderful escargots…" Ethan encouraged her.

"No, really, I'm not that hungry."

"I'll pass as well and I'll let you know when we are ready to order dinner."

The server nodded and left, leaving Sophie to continue with her less than dignified apology.

"Feel free to continue with your apology." Ethan's comment irritated Sophie which she supposed was the purpose.

"Okay, well you see, my family…" She hesitated. She was afraid to tell him about their hotel connection. She was positive he would become alarmed.

"Your family, what?"

"You know when your father told me you owned the Tuxedo line of hotels?"

"Yes, what of it?"

"Well, I wasn't exactly sure how to respond to that." She was being as cautious as possible.

"Why?" Ethan never took his eyes off her as he sipped on his wine.

"Because..."

"Ethan?! Is that you?"

Looking around Sophie was astounded to see a gorgeous, tall woman walk up to their table. She had long, straight, blond hair, parted in the middle, precisely placed behind her ears. She had to have been almost six feet tall in heels and had a figure that any woman would be envious of. Her make-up was impeccably done and she wore long, dangly earrings which Sophie speculated were diamonds, that sparkled in the light. Her nails were long and perfectly manicured and Sophie couldn't help but notice the stunning red strapless dress that was perfectly fitted to her figure and complimented with a white shoulder shawl.

"What are you doing here?" She glanced at Sophie with a scrutinizing look then turned her attention to Ethan, who politely stood to greet the woman who hugged him then kissed him on the lips.

Sophie's eyebrows raised in surprise.

"I thought you had a business meeting tonight?"

"I do."

Sophie noticed that Ethan maintained his composure as he addressed the woman.

I wonder who this is? His girlfriend perhaps? Most likely, given the kiss on the lips but that would be rather uncomfortable. He never mentioned he had a girlfriend although, he doesn't answer to me, but you would think he would have said something about a girlfriend if that were the case.

"Addison, this is Ms..." Realizing he never did know Sophie's last name, he changed course. "This is Sophie. Sophie, this is Addison Chambers-Goldman."

Sophie went to speak but was quickly dismissed by the woman.

"I want to speak to you privately...now!"

Her indifference was evident and Sophie certainly didn't want to get in the middle of whatever was happening here.

"I'll leave. I need to go to the ladies room anyway." Grabbing her purse, Sophie quickly stood up and was mortified to have everything in her purse fall out onto the floor. Kneeling on the floor, Sophie frantically grabbed what she could, stuffing it back in her purse. She could feel the piercing glare of Addison without even having to look. Reaching around Addison's feet and under the table, Sophie managed to collect everything. Trying to stand back up, she took hold of the chair and pulled herself up to attention. Wiggling her dress back down into place, she glanced over to Ethan who looked very sympathetic, then over to Addison who looked completely indifferent to her struggles.

Oh my God! That was just a tad humiliating.

Walking away, she heard Addison ask, "Who is that woman, Ethan? I'm your fiancée. I deserve to know what is...?"

That was all she heard before stopping a server to point her in the direction of the washroom. Standing in the washroom, Sophie was trying to process what she had overheard.

Peeking out the washroom door towards their table, she saw Addison very animatedly speaking with Ethan, who at this moment was doing very little talking.

Fiancée! What the hell? That was awkward. Now what do I do? Stay in the washroom and for how long? Better yet, I should just leave.

Retrieving her coat, Sophie opened up her purse to grab her phone and became dismayed when she realized that it wasn't there and assumed it was somewhere on the floor near their table. She couldn't go home now.

Looking around, trying to figure out where to go, Sophie spotted the lounge near the entrance and decided that was the place.

Walking up to the bar, she ordered a glass of red wine then found a small easy chair in front of the fireplace and sat down. She had no intention of going back to that table until Addison was gone. Who knows how long that would be and she didn't care. She knew she couldn't leave but also didn't want to be in the line of fire. Let Ethan explain his way out of his little indiscretion.

She was almost finished her wine when she looked up to see Ethan standing in the bar entrance. Seeing Sophie, he walked over and sat down, placing her phone on the table in front of her.

"I'm sorry about that. Addison can be rather…shall I say, possessive."

Sophie wasn't sure what to say. It really wasn't any of her business.

"She's gone now."

"Who is she? Your…"

"*Not* fiancée." Ethan abruptly interrupted. "Although I have a hard time getting her to understand that." Thinking for a moment, Ethan said, "I mean, we have been together…"

"So, she *is* your fiancée then." Sophie didn't understand why she was annoyed but she had to admit that she was surprisingly angry to think he had a girlfriend and even worse, a fiancée and hadn't mentioned anything about her.

"No…well, sort of…there is nothing set in stone." He fumbled for the right words.

"She either is or she isn't." Sophie pursued the conversation. "Not that it's any of my business. If you need to go with her, please, don't let me stop you."

"No, I don't need to go with her." Ethan was adamant.

"Seems to me like you should. You lied to her and said you had a business meeting. Why?"

"As I mentioned, she's rather possessive. She wouldn't understand..."

Sophie was confused by her feelings. He was nothing to her. Why did this all bother her so much?

She nodded, "I see...well...I really don't see." She couldn't look Ethan in the eyes. She felt surprisingly...hurt. Actually, very hurt by his lack of disclosure.

Sophie picked up her phone and stuffed it in her purse.

"I should go." Standing to leave, she put on her coat.

"Please don't." Ethan quickly stood up.

"No, I better go. This feels extremely uncomfortable." Sophie turned to leave.

"Sophie, wait."

She felt Ethan's hand gently grab her arm to stop her. Standing with her back to him she waited.

"Sophie."

Turning to face Ethan, Sophie waited for him to continue. Placing his hands tenderly on either side of her face, he kissed her so passionately on the lips and with such intensity that it aroused a desire within her that she had never felt with anyone before.

Mindlessly dropping her purse onto the floor, she pulled away and stared into his eyes trying to understand what was happening.

"Ethan..."

Kissing her again, Ethan gently placed his arms around her waist, pulling her close to his firm, strong body. His kiss was seductive with a provocativeness that created such overwhelming sexual feelings in her that she simply couldn't resist and shamelessly reciprocated.

Within moments Sophie reluctantly pulled herself away, finding herself breathless. With her hand she pushed hair away from her face as she tried to regain her composure. "Ethan, we can't..."

"We can, Sophie."

"I have to go. Picking up her purse, Sophie hastily left the restaurant. Tears hindered her vision and she tripped over the door mat, losing her right shoe in the process. Stopping briefly, she quickly picked it up and put it back on, hopping along on one foot as she did so. She spoke to the valet, who nodded, then flagged down a taxi.

By the time Ethan caught up to her, he helplessly watched as she slammed the door shut and drove off.

TWENTY ONE

Arriving in her suite, Sophie closed the door behind her and let out a sigh of relief. Standing there, she was unsure of what to think. She was shocked and confused by what just took place and even more so by her feelings. The smell of his cologne still lingered on her.

That was so unexpected. What the hell just happened? The attraction was undeniable but also just simply wrong. I mean, he has a fiancée. A fiancée!! How could he kiss me like that and be engaged to someone else? It was all wrong, and yet…I desperately wanted to run back to him but knew I couldn't…shouldn't.

Thinking further, she grew angry.

How could he do that? How could he kiss me so passionately when he's engaged? Right after his fiancée just left. He had no qualms about it, either. What the hell is wrong with that guy?

She wasn't sure how long she stood there before hearing her phone ring. She knew it would be Ethan trying to call her again. She ignored it. She couldn't speak with him right now. This was more than she could deal with. She was on an emotional rollercoaster and felt like her whole world was spinning out of control. She was angry yet her feelings for him were rapidly evolving; exposing an undeniable attraction.

Kicking her heels off, Sophie walked into the bedroom and changed into leggings and a sweatshirt. Pulling her hair down, she walked into the living room in her bare feet, poured herself a glass of wine from the bar fridge and sat out on the balcony staring mindlessly at the city lights. She listened to the sounds of sirens blaring and horns honking while a gentle breeze softly swept through her hair. She could hear her phone ringing several times in the living room where she left it. She needed time to think, to process what just took place between her and Ethan.

I've never felt like that before...with anyone.

Her heart skipped a beat at the thought of his passionate kiss, the way he looked at her, held her with such tenderness, the smell of his cologne. There was a connection that she had never experienced...ever.

Hearing the phone ring once again, Sophie closed her eyes, willing herself not to weaken and answer because if she did, she couldn't say no to him. Something inside her unlocked the floodgates of her heart when he kissed her. One of the hardest things she ever had to do was walk away from him. However, if she were to give in now, she would never forgive herself.

Eventually, the phone stopped ringing. She was grateful. Sitting out on the balcony until she could no longer keep her eyes open, Sophie finally crawled into bed and slept.

TWENTY TWO

THE NEXT MORNING, SOPHIE AWOKE exhausted, both physically and emotionally. She hadn't slept well. Lying in bed, she stared at the ceiling contemplating what to do about Ethan and replaying in her mind what occurred last evening.

Over the next few days, she avoided all calls from Ethan. Eventually he just stopped calling. She was grateful he didn't come by the hotel to see her. She decided it was best to put it all behind her for now and focus on getting her mother's estate sorted out.

By the end of the week, she received a phone call from Mr. Hawthorne with the news she was waiting to hear.

"My client has finally gotten back to me. Well, it wasn't my client directly, it was their assistant. They have asked for an extension to be able to deal with things appropriately at their end."

"Oh, I see." Sophie was hoping to get this all finalized sooner than later. This was not the news she had hoped to receive but there was nothing that could be done.

"Yes, of course. How long do they require?"

"They have requested another week, approximately. It might be sooner."

"Mr. Hawthorne, why do they need that long? Why can't they deal with it now? I don't understand."

"Apparently, something unexpected arose this week and they were unable to sit down and address matters."

Sighing, Sophie didn't have the energy to argue.

"My preference would have been to have everything finalized by the end of this month...but, I suppose one more week shouldn't be an issue. That's fine."

"Very well. I will pass that along to my client. Thank you."

"I look forward to getting this settled."

"Of course."

"Oh, and Mr. Hawthorne?"

"Yes?"

"Explain to your client that I am getting pushed at my end to get this finalized. We have details to sort out here as well and the sooner your client can meet the better. We did, after all, request the end of October."

"Understood. I will pass that along, Ms Callaghan."

Hanging up the phone, Sophie was trying to decide whether to go home, which would solve any possibility of her running into Ethan again, or to stay in the hopes that she would be able to wrap things up sooner. She was emotionally very tired.

Picking up the phone, she called the office and spoke to Tony.

"Tony, I'm going to stay out here a week or two longer. I can work remotely. I do have my laptop. Meetings we can handle through video conferencing. How are things going there?"

"Just fine, Sophie. No big issues that haven't been dealt with by others. You really do need to attend a meeting or two which are coming up, though. I have been able to hold people off these last couple of weeks but otherwise I think that it will become problematic."

"Okay, send me the details via email and I'll look everything over. Any meetings that need to take place, book them for next Friday and let's have them all on the same day."

"Will do, oh, and Sophie?"

"Yes?"

"Francine has been calling."

"Remember, do not give her or Tyler my new mobile number. I can't deal with their drama right now. I've got enough of my own."

"Absolutely."

"Thanks, Tony." The last thing Sophie needed was Francine and Tyler pressuring her.

"Okay, so, I've just emailed all the information you require for your meetings. There is a lot to read so, vacation is over." Tony chuckled.

"That was rather quick."

"I had it ready to go."

"You were so sure I would agree to this."

"No doubt in my mind." Tony chuckled.

"Okay, I'll get to it today and if there is anything else, you know how to get ahold of me."

Hanging up from Tony, she was grateful for his dedication and loyalty. Tony Moretti had been her assistant for almost five years, starting when she was Vice President. Then when her parents had both died, and she took over as CEO, she brought Tony along with her. There was no one more efficient. He was worth his weight in gold as far as Sophie was concerned. She could trust him with her life.

Grabbing her laptop, she hunkered down with a coffee and got to work. It felt good to have something to do that would distract her from all the complications of her life.

TWENTY THREE

THE NEXT WEEK WENT BY quickly and Sophie was relieved she hadn't heard from Ethan. It was one complication too many right now. Regardless, she couldn't get him off her mind. It didn't matter what she was doing, her thoughts would drift to him, his kiss, her heart. She desperately wanted to see him again but whenever she thought of him being engaged, she grew angry at the thought that he never mentioned it to her.

She really was a bitch if you ask me but I suppose if I had found my fiancée out to dinner with another woman, I wouldn't exactly be on my best behaviour either. What a shock for her. And does she even know about the other times we were together? It's not like anything happened but that isn't the point now is it? He wasn't upfront about it…with either of us.

Shaking herself from her thoughts, Sophie started to get some work done. The man had already taken up far too much of her time. Opening her laptop she began typing up an email to Tony.

And to expect me to just ignore the fact that he's engaged. To brush it off like it was nothing. And then to kiss me the way he did. I mean, the nerve!

Sitting daydreaming, Sophie thought back to that moment.

So unexpected. His kiss was…amazing…the passion. My God…I have to admit, he took my breath away.

"Enough! What the hell is wrong with me? He's engaged. I won't be seeing him again, anyway. It's done."

Just then her phone rang and she looked and saw that it was an unknown number.

"Hello?"

"Sophie, my dear, how are you?"

"Winston. What a surprise." Sophie was reluctant to have a conversation with him as well. The hotel situation was problematic and she certainly didn't want to be accused of trying to get information from this man.

"I was hoping you could come for a visit this weekend. I'm feeling much better and of course, I would expect you to join me for dinner."

"I would love to Winston, however, I've got some business to take care of. I'm really rather busy."

"Surely you can take a few hours out of your day and visit an old man who has been housebound. I would very much appreciate the company."

"I'm sorry. I just can't. Another time perhaps, before I head home again."

"Very well. I will hold you to that." Winston sounded disappointed but understanding.

"I promise." Sophie really didn't want to take the chance that Ethan would be there, let alone the idea of work coming up.

Hanging up from Winston, Sophie got back to the task at hand. She needed to prepare for the upcoming meetings that afternoon.

Closing her laptop, Sophie rested back on the chair.

"My God, that was a whirlwind of meetings but thankfully they are done and over with for this week. I think I've earned dinner albeit an early one."

Changing into yoga pants and a pullover sweater, Sophie took the elevator to the lobby. She was already planning what she would have for dinner. She was starving. Stepping off the elevator she headed to the restaurant. Passing through the lobby she stopped cold.

"Ethan."

"Sophie."

"What are you doing here? How did you know I'd even be here right now."

"I took a chance and waited, hoping you would come down to eat. I need to talk to you and you wouldn't answer any of my calls."

"Of course not. What did you expect?" She instantly grew angry. "My God, Ethan, you're engaged. What the hell did you think you were doing? You can't just mess with peoples' emotions like that."

"Sophie, I can explain. It's not what you think."

He took a step towards her. Her heart fluttered, her palms grew sweaty.

"Explain what…," She grew flustered and began fidgeting with her necklace, trying to maintain her defences. "What exactly is it then?" She had a hard time gathering her thoughts.

"Just give me a chance to explain."

Looking away, Sophie tried to redirect her thoughts by looking at people coming and going past them, carrying on with their own lives oblivious to what Sophie was dealing with. She was, at this very moment, having a very difficult time reining in her emotions.

People were arriving with luggage, there were people at the front desk arranging for their rooms, some sitting talking quietly to one another.

She could hear phones quietly ringing, the sound of wheels on the luggage carts trundling along the marble floors, elevators indicating their arrival at the lobby.

Looking back at Ethan, she caught her breath. He was now standing directly in front of her, close enough to touch, if she wanted. She could smell his cologne.

Oh my God. Sophie struggled to focus.

He was right there. Close enough to kiss…if she so desired…and boy did she desire. Every part of her desired. She wanted to make mad, passionate love with him. She had never felt this way about anyone before. Yes, she had men in her life but none made her feel the way Ethan did. It was unsettling.

That damn cologne…he smells so good.

Forcing herself to take a step back, Sophie momentarily closed her eyes and took a deep breath in. Dropping her room key, she couldn't will herself to move. She could barely contain her emotions as she felt his arm brush along hers as he reached down to pick it up for her.

Oh my God. Give me the strength…

"Ethan, I think it would be best if we didn't see each other."

"Sophie, you don't understand."

"Then explain it to me."

"Please, can we go somewhere private?"

Looking around, Sophie recommended the lounge across the lobby from the restaurant.

Finding a private corner, they ordered drinks.

"So, what's to explain, Ethan? Really, it seems pretty clear to me." Sophie had collected her thoughts and readied herself for a conversation she had hoped wouldn't happen. "Are you engaged or aren't you?"

"You see, well…no…sort of."

"Sort of?" Sophie was skeptical.

"It's complicated."

"Not from where I am, it's not. Ethan, I refuse to get in between you and…and…"

"Addison."

"…Addison. Not that I'm a fan…she's rather snooty if you ask me but hey, maybe that works for you."

"Well, no…" Ethan was having a hard time getting a word in.

"Well anyway, you need to deal with that whole scenario before you ever consider whatever took place between us…which…by the way, admittedly, was rather…nice…"

Ethan smiled.

"BUT…should never have happened." Sophie tried to maintain the virtual wall she had put up between them. It was the only way she could contain her emotions.

"And, how dare you kiss me like that!"

"Like what?" Ethan looked confused.

"Like…like…with such passion…you have some nerve!"

Sophie knew she was losing her stance in the conversation although it had been pretty much a one-sided conversation anyway. Ethan sat waiting for Sophie to stop talking long enough for him to speak.

"I mean…you just don't realize it, do you?"

"Realize what?" Again Ethan was having difficulty understanding what was happening.

"And that cologne…"

"What does my cologne have to do with this?" Ethan shook his head, confused.

"Oh, never mind!" Sophie knew she had to leave or lose to her heart. Standing up rather clumsily, she knocked her drink all over the table.

"Dammit!" Grabbing napkins, she started to wipe up the spill but just as she leaned in to do so, Ethan also leaned in to wipe the mess when their foreheads hit.

"Ow! Oh my God, I have to leave." Dropping the napkins on the table, Sophie signed off the bar bill with her name and suite number then grabbed her room key. She was hungry and irritated and now her head hurt.

"You know what, Ethan? Don't bother calling me. I've got enough happening in my life right now and I don't need another complication."

"Sophie, oh my God, It's not that complicated. Why are you being so pig-headed?"

"Pig-headed! Pig-headed? You have some nerve suggesting that I'm be-ing pig-headed! I wasn't the one who started this whole...this whole... thing!"

"And what is that supposed to mean?"

"Good-bye, Ethan. Say hello to your dad for me." She didn't dare look back. "And go home to your fiancée." She practically spit the words out as she walked away.

"I came here to explain things. You're the one who refuses to listen! So, yeah, you're being pig-headed," he shouted after her.

What the hell just happened? He's got some nerve!! I came here to deal with an estate matter, not fall in love, if that's what you want to call this. I mean, I'm sure it's not love...it couldn't be.

Stopping in the lobby trying to decide what to do with herself, she was furious. She decided to go back to her suite and order in room service. She wasn't in the mood to be surrounded by people.

"He's absolutely infuriating! How dare he call me pig-headed! He's the one who is cheating on his fiancée, not me! I never asked for this, never asked to be kissed by him. I mean, who the hell does he think he is?"

Thinking about how she'd felt when he'd kissed her, then when she'd seen him tonight, something inside of her told her that if she were to let him out of her life, she would regret it, but...there was the matter of Addison.

No, I'm not going there. I need to focus and get things sorted out and then go home. I can't believe I allowed that bloody guy to get under my skin. He's infuriating! And besides, he's too old for me anyway...not to mention...he's short tempered, if his outburst at the hospital is any evidence...

Sophie tried to reason with her emotions.

...and besides, his cologne isn't all that great, anyway.

Pondering that thought, she decided to retract it.

Oh, who am I kidding? His cologne really is amazing!

Within moments, there was a knock at her door. Still angry, she abruptly opened it. Seeing Ethan standing there infuriated her and she went to close the door again. She almost had it shut when he shouted out to her.

"I broke it off with Addison."

Skeptical she asked, "When did you have time to do that? We were just talking..."

"This week. I had been trying to get a hold of her ever since that night we were at Frigo's. She eventually returned my call. We talked, we fought. I broke it off, not that there was really anything to break off."

Questioning her decision, Sophie opened the door back up, not fully trusting what he was telling her.

"What a shitty thing to do, break off an engagement over the phone!" Sophie wasn't impressed but inside she was thrilled to hear the news.

"True. It was a shitty thing to do." Ethan couldn't disagree.

"She must have been furious."

"To say the least."

"She likely blames me."

"Entirely blames you, actually."

"Is that why you're here? To tell me."

"It is."

"And what do you expect to happen now?"

"This."

Walking in, Ethan kissed her with such passion and tenderness that she immediately melted in his arms. Slamming the door shut with her foot, Sophie continued kissing him. Pushing Ethan back against the wall, Sophie pressed her body against his. Her body tingled under his touch as his hands reached under her sweater working their way up her back to her bra. Undoing it, Ethan then worked his hands around to her breasts. She became breathless and momentarily stopped kissing him. She melted with his gentle touch as he caressed her nipples. Leaning in to kiss him, Sophie felt her legs weaken as he worked his hands down to her yoga pants. Slowly slipping his hands in, he began massaging between her legs.

Ethan picked her up and Sophie straddled his body with her legs as he carried her into the bedroom and gently laid her onto the bed. Ethan slipped her pants off as she helped him remove his shirt. Quickly undressing, Ethan slid himself into Sophie with methodical almost frantic movements and within moments they shuddered together in ecstasy. Sophie couldn't help but moan in appreciation. Ethan leaned down and kissed her on the lips, then her neck, working his way to her nipples where he massaged them with his tongue.

"Oh my God, Ethan..." Sophie looked up and leaned in to kiss him and they made passionate love once again.

Lying in each others arms, breathless and exhausted Sophie couldn't help but question what was happening between them.

This seems like a dream...I can't believe I'm lying here right now...like this...with him. Is this a hookup...or something more?

"Ethan?"

"Yeah?"

"I can't have one more complication in my life right now..."

Rolling onto his side to face Sophie, Ethan asked, "What do you mean?"

"What I mean is..." She wasn't entirely sure what she wanted herself. "What is this for you?"

"I don't understand."

"I'm not interested in a hook up if that's what this is."

Lying quietly, Ethan didn't respond immediately and Sophie became concerned.

"I'm not necessarily looking for marriage either," she clarified.

Watching as Ethan just nodded and seemed to be contemplating what she said, she wasn't sure if it was a good thing, or not.

"Although I wouldn't say it's outside the realm of possibility. I've just never felt you need to get married to prove how you feel about someone. And it's not to say that I expect to get married, God no! I mean, we barely know each other. It's also not to say that I'm a one night stand kind of a girl either. No sirree! I mean, I've had the odd one night stand and I know that it isn't for me so if that's what this is, then I'm out which makes no sense since...you know...we've already had it...

Taking a moment to think through what she wanted to say, Sophie added, "Let's face it, we just met. Maybe you think you like me and you get to know me better and then find out you actually hate me, that's a very real possibility. I've had that happen before too, except it was me hating the guy..."

"Sophie, would you please just stop talking." Ethan pleaded.

"Pardon?"

"You need to just stop talking."

"Well, that's offensive."

I know I was rambling and can't blame him for telling me to shut up. I hate when I ramble like this. It always happens when I'm excited or nervously uncomfortable...if that's even a term.

"Sophie."

"What?" She became apprehensive.

"Let's be very clear."

Here it comes. The ole you were great, this was great but I'm just not that interested in anything long term. Just like that Clint guy back in university. What a jerk he was.

"This is not a hook-up but this is not about getting married either, although, like you, it isn't outside the realm of possibility...sometime down the road when we know each other better...if we decide that's what we want..."

"Okay." Sophie waited for what she was sure to be the bombshell being dropped.

"This is entirely about you and I being attracted to each other right here, right now. I really care about you. I want to be with you."

"Oh." Sophie wasn't sure what she had expected him to say but it wasn't that. "Okay."

"I want to be with you…for, hopefully, a very long time."

"Okay."

"And if you feel the same way then I think we have established what 'this' is, wouldn't you agree?" Ethan had kept his eyes on Sophie the entire time he was talking.

The sincerity was evident and Sophie soon relaxed, understanding that Ethan really was different from all the other men she had dated.

"I would agree." Sophie smiled then leaned in and kissed him.

Getting up to dress, Sophie had to ask. "So, what happened with Addison?"

"Addison and I weren't really engaged."

"What the hell does that mean?"

"Well, we were, in her mind. She proposed, I never accepted. In fact, I never answered and she took that as a yes. I tried to explain to her many times…she's a very determined woman." Ethan shook his head. "Don't get me wrong, we have dated for a couple of years now. Well, dated is a rather strong word…more like we attended events together and people made the assumption that we were a couple. I just never bothered to correct them. I didn't care enough."

Getting out of bed, Ethan spoke as he began to get dressed.

"You should have. There really is no excuse. That wasn't exactly fair to Addison." *Not that I really care. She's a snooty bitch.*

Ethan nodded, "True."

"I mean, I'd trash you all over town if you did that to me." *Bit of an overstatement.*

"Fair enough. I'll be sure to keep that in mind."

Sophie watched as Ethan put on his shirt, covering his well built physique. *Jeez, he's damn hot.*

"But at the time…"

"At the time, what?" Sophie drew her thoughts back to the conversation.

"At the time, there was no one I cared about, so I ran with it."

"And now?" Sophie wanted to hear him say it.

"And now…I have someone I care about."

"Given your recent history, don't you think you should be sure the other person feels the same way?" Sophie gave him a scrutinizing look.

Having put on his pants, Ethan walked over to Sophie and wrapped his arms around her.

"I'm pretty sure she does." Leaning in, he tenderly kissed her.

"I'm pretty sure you're right." Sophie melted. "Although, admittedly, you are kind of robbing the cradle, don't you think?"

"A shot to my heart…how could you say that?"

"I give you full credit though, you were not at all like an old man in your love making…not that I've ever made love to an old man to know for sure." Sophie chuckled.

Walking over to put his shoes on, Ethan just grinned.

"How do you know I'm not some gold-digger after your money?" Sophie teased.

"I don't, but I'll take my chances."

"Do you want to get some food?" Sophie was still quite hungry.

"You go ahead, I need to head out. I have an important meeting to attend and I'm running late as it is. Then I should be catching up with Dad, if it's not too late. He wanted to speak to me about something."

"What are you going to tell him about us? Will he be disappointed about Addison?"

"I'll figure it out when the time comes. Quite frankly, he never liked Addison anyway and she never liked him. He seems to have a soft spot for you though. Something about saving his life…"

Ethan kissed Sophie good-bye. "I'll call you later."

Shutting the door behind him, Sophie leaned back against the door and smiled.

I really do love his cologne…and his body isn't so bad either.

TWENTY FOUR

SOPHIE EXPECTED TO HEAR FROM Ethan later that evening but he never called and by the next evening she was getting concerned and tried to call him but to no avail.

I wonder if he's had second thoughts. I mean it is entirely possible. It was rather sudden after all.

Dialling his number once again, Sophie was disappointed there was no answer.

"Ethan, it's Sophie. Please call."

By Monday morning, Sophie grew concerned that she still hadn't heard from Ethan. Fortunately, her attention was diverted away from her relationship troubles with a phone call from Mr. Hawthorne.

"Ms Callaghan, I have some news."

"I'm glad to hear this, Mr. Hawthorne. What have you heard?" Sophie was torn between excitement and nerves.

"Just a quick update. I spoke to my client and they have been unable to get things sorted out at their end. If you could be patient."

"Mr. Hawthorne, there is a deadline and we have already extended it."

"There is something coming up that is taking priority, if you will. Just another week, could be sooner."

Giving it some thought, Sophie didn't think it would hurt to give them another week, although she certainly couldn't figure out what could possibly be so important that they couldn't meet about such a life changing conversation, although, to be fair, she realized that they weren't aware of the details.

"That's fine, Mr. Hawthorne."

"Thank you. My client has said that this will be the last extension."

"Thank you for all your efforts, Mr. Hawthorne. It will be nice to get this all finalized for my mother."

"I'm sure it will. We will be in touch, Ms Callaghan."

Hanging up from Mr. Hawthorne, Sophie opted to try calling Ethan once more.

"Hello?"

"Ethan, I've been trying to call you. What's going on?"

"There were some unexpected issues with Addison that have kept me busy. I'm sorry, Sophie, I should have returned your call."

Sophie didn't want to pry. She wanted to give Ethan his privacy but, admittedly, she wondered what could possibly have happened with Addison.

"Are you having second thoughts about us?" Sophie hated to even ask the question.

"Not at all, although, I do need to tell you that Addison and I are committed to attending a fundraiser this Saturday night and it would be detrimental to the charity if we weren't to attend together. We have been spearheading this charity for years now and finally have an opportunity to bring together significant donors to help the cause."

"Really? So, you have to go and pretend to be engaged?" Sophie didn't like the sound of this at all.

"Well, no...yes, actually. I hope you understand."

"Well, actually, I don't understand. Why can't you just give up the charade that you're engaged. What does it matter?"

"It's not that simple, Sophie."

"Oh, I think it is, Ethan. So, you ignore my calls all weekend, you don't call me back and now you tell me that you have to attend this event under the guise of being Addison's fiancé and you expect me to just... understand."

"Yes, yes, I do."

"I think that's an unreasonable request."

"Well, I think you're being stubborn and not seeing the whole picture." Ethan was growing impatient.

"Is that right?" Sophie was angry. "You can think what you want, Ethan, but I don't see why you need to keep up this little charade unless..."

"Unless what?"

"Unless you want to."

"That's utterly ridiculous, Sophie! Of course I don't want to pretend I'm engaged. This is only for one night. Why is it so difficult for you to comprehend that this is bigger than you and I or even Addison for that matter? It's a major charitable auction looking to raise millions of dollars. We have worked on this for a very long time and I'm not willing to risk donors walking away because they don't see Addison and me as being stable in our own relationship."

"What has that got to do with anything?"

"The fact that, Addison and I have set this charity up and we both sit on the board of directors. If our donors don't think we can maintain our own relationship, they may not think we can maintain stability within our own charity if they find out we are no longer together. We need to offer stability from the top down until such time as we can transition responsibility to others."

"That's bullshit and you know it." Sophie found his reasoning completely laughable. "Who talked you into that ridiculous line of reasoning? Addison?"

"You know what, Sophie? This weekend hasn't exactly been stellar for me and I don't need to argue my rationalization nor my principles surrounding my decisions about this fundraiser with you or anyone else. I need to do this and I was hoping you would have respected that. You are obviously too young and inexperienced to understand the importance of such things."

"What the hell?! Are you seriously that condescending?"

"It's not about being condescending, it's just an observation...

"You are one seriously patronizing son-of-a-bitch!"

"I thought you would understand but clearly I was wrong."

"Clearly you were." Sophie was so angry she couldn't control what she was saying.

"Feel free to be engaged to Addison again, Ethan. It's your life and I suppose I was fooling myself to think you were different. And for your information, you don't know me nor what my experience is, so you can take that ageist bias of yours and shove it up your ass!"

Hanging up the phone before Ethan could respond, Sophie began to cry. How quickly the tables had turned.

I think it's time I get this estate business sorted out and go home. I can't believe I allowed myself to get involved with someone so incapable of separating his personal life from business and someone so unbelievably condescending and arrogant. What a bunch of bullshit!

Hearing her phone ring, Sophie checked to see if it was Ethan calling her back and was relieved to see that it wasn't. She was still too angry to have a reasonable conversation with him.

"Hi Tony, what's up?" It took all her strength to control the tears and keep her voice strong.

"I've been getting calls from Francine demanding I tell her where you are, or at the very least, provide her with your mobile."

"Don't do it, Tony, or you're fired." Sophie wasn't serious about firing him but she was absolutely serious that she did not want any contact with her sister. "I just can't deal with her right now. Things have become far more problematic than I had anticipated."

"Are you okay? You sound upset?"

The man knows me all too well.

Clearing her throat, Sophie said, "No, I'm fine, just needed to clear my throat."

"Ah okay. So, is there anything I can do to help you with all of this?"

Tony had always been there to fix any problem that had ever crossed Sophie's path. He was a wiz at resolving them but Sophie knew this was one thing she had to take care of on her own.

"I'll keep you posted. If this situation with my mother's estate gets to drag on much longer then I just may need your assistance."

"Have you met with the family yet?"

"No, apparently they have had a bit of a glitch at their end. They have requested more time."

"I'm sure you are not exactly singing your mother praises right about now."

Tony's relationship with Sophie was more than just your average business relationship and he knew almost all there was to know about Sophie's personal life.

"Oh, you are so right, Tony. You knew my mother. She was one head-strong woman and I can only imagine that she knew exactly how difficult this would be to deal with."

"She was a remarkable woman, Sophie. You will do her proud, I know it."

"Thanks Tony. I'll keep you posted and remember, do not give my number or location to my sister, under any circumstances."

"I know, I know. No worries. She won't get anything out of me. I just keep pleading ignorance. You are away, you didn't say where you were going, I'm not at liberty to give out your personal mobile number."

"Talk soon." Sophie hung up the phone and was at a loss as to what to do next. She was furious with Ethan and was at a standstill regarding her mother's estate.

I can't believe what an arrogant asshole he was. How dare he suggest I'm too young to understand the extent of his situation. How dare he assume I'm too young to have any relevant experience. Bastard!

To say she was livid was an understatement. Sophie had no interest in talking to him now or ever again. Emotional collateral damage clearly wasn't an issue for him.

TWENTY FIVE

THE NEXT EVENING, SOPHIE WAS disappointed in herself having moped all day in her hotel room doing nothing but tormenting herself about what Ethan had said.

Oh, I have no doubt he will play the game just exactly as it needs to be played. How would his donors feel if they ever found out the whole thing was a sham? Surely that would be a far more difficult conversation to have than to admit that they weren't engaged.

Sophie finally changed and wandered down to the lobby to hit the coffee shop. Seeing Anika at the front desk speaking to the concierge, Sophie waved hello.

Anika waved to Sophie then signalled that she would be over in a moment. Finally nodding to the concierge, Anika walked over and sat down on an easy chair opposite Sophie in the lobby.

"Good evening, Sophie. How are you doing?"

"Hello Anika. Busy day?"

"Yes, as a matter of fact, we have a large party checking-in first thing Sunday morning. Students, and I wanted Serge to ensure that the porters were all available to work to get luggage to rooms quickly. How are you doing? I've been off visiting the other hotels ensuring things are running as they should. What have you been doing while I've been gone?"

Anika smiled her signature warm smile which relaxed Sophie. Anika always had a way of making someone feel like everything would be okay, even when things were at their worst.

"I had a rather upsetting day yesterday. I met someone and unfortunately, it isn't working out."

"I'm sorry to hear that. What happened? Can I help?" Anika's concern was genuine.

"I thought he was a great guy but his true colours showed through." Sophie thought for a moment. "Have you ever heard of Ethan Blackburn?"

"Yes, of course. His father owns the Tuxedo chain of hotels. Is that who you have been seeing?"

"I have."

"I heard he was engaged."

"He is...was...I don't really know." Sophie was so confused by it all. "He's not really, but he pretends to be, which is partly why it didn't work out. He seemed like a great guy but then we argued over this auction event he and his...supposed fiancée...Addison, are putting on this Saturday and well..."

"Does he realize who you are?" Anika was surprised by what she was hearing.

"No, not at all, thank God. It just never came up in conversation."

"That's pretty important information to share. You wouldn't want him thinking you are interested because of his position."

"True, but it doesn't really matter now. We had an argument. His arrogance..."

"You know he's actually not an arrogant person. I've met him and he's actually a very sweet man."

"I find that hard to believe." Sophie knew she would need some convincing.

"He's a real philanthropist. From time to time he chooses and supports one charitable organization, working with them to create awareness and developing programs to assist those individuals who utilize those organizations. Not to mention that he uses his influence to solicit donations from those he knows, who have the resources to put into these programs. As you can well imagine, money is a big worry for these charities and Ethan Blackburn breaks those walls down and encourages corporations and wealthy individuals to invest in them. He's extremely good at it."

"Really?"

"Most definitely. A few years ago, he decided to raise funds for an orphanage in Africa called Omolara that had been struggling to meet the needs of the children in their care. Ethan and Addison had a tour of the orphanage at that time, met with the director and staff, then proceeded to take a couple of weeks to help out and meet the children who live there. Within these last few years, he has solicited donated funds from his contacts to allow the orphanage to continue to operate and extended it to include an adoption agency. It's now called Omolara Orphanage and Adoption Agency. Through his contacts in the trades industry, he managed to have tradesmen donate their time to go over and renovate much of the orphanage that is falling to ruin. I'm telling you, Sophie, the man is a gem."

Sophie was dumbfounded.

"He's so private. He never mentioned any of this. Well, he mentioned he had been working with a charity for a couple of years now and has a fundraiser coming up."

"He is a very private person when it comes to his charity work. He doesn't do this for his own glory. This is all about the organizations he helps, not about him helping them. Don't hold his discretion against him. It's really to protect the organizations he supports."

"So he expressed, and I so poorly responded to." Sophie suddenly felt extremely disgusted by her behaviour. Maybe Ethan was correct.

"He suggested I was too young and inexperienced to understand..."

"Oh now, you don't believe that, do you?" Anika looked at Sophie with kindness.

"After my behaviour yesterday? I am now wondering..." Sophie contemplated the possibility.

"Now, Sophie. Don't you ever question your ability to deal with very difficult life matters. You have always been more than capable. Don't doubt that. I'm sure whatever you said to each other was spoken out of anger and not because either of you truly believed it."

"I've completely embarrassed myself, Anika, and as you say, I've not had an opportunity to explain who I am to him. I'm afraid that now, it will put into jeopardy whatever slight chance we may have had for a relationship, if yesterday hasn't already. Which I'm sure it has. How could it not?"

"I'm sure you will figure out what to do. You are a very clever woman, I have faith in you. You are much like your mother, Sophie. She too was a woman who set her mind to something and refused to give up until she accomplished what she wanted to do."

Anika stood up and put her hand on Sophie's shoulder.

"You will work this out, I've no doubt."

Looking up at Anika, Sophie was at a loss to know how she was going to work things out but Anika seemed to think she could.

"Thanks for listening, Anika. Have I ever told you that if I had a sister, I would want her to be just like you?"

"You have." Anika grinned. "And each time I must remind you that you have a sister."

The two women laughed and Sophie smiled as she watched Anika walk towards the front desk, nodding to the clerk, who was desperately trying to get her attention.

Grabbing her coffee and sandwich from the coffee shop, Sophie headed back to her suite. She was contemplating what she could do to fix the entire situation with Ethan.

Curled up in a chair, Sophie watched TV and spent the evening mulling over possibilities of how she could make amends for her bad behaviour.

By the next morning she was frustrated, at having spent so much time trying to figure out a solution with no luck, when suddenly it hit her.

"Oh my God! That's it!"

TWENTY SIX

Picking up the hotel phone, Sophie dialled a familiar extension.

"Anika Patel."

"Anika, I need your help."

Hanging up from her conversation with Anika, Sophie waited patiently for a return call which she received an hour later with further details.

Receiving the information she needed from Anika, Sophie called Tony and explained what she needed to happen, and why.

"Tony, I need you to contact the board of directors and get them to approve something for me, and it has to be by the end of the day tomorrow. They must do it by conference call and/or email, whichever works to get this done."

"My God, Sophie! You are asking the impossible. You know how difficult it is to get hold of these people on a good day let alone for an emergency motion for approval."

"You have almost a full two days. I know you can do this, Tony. You've never let me down."

"You know I dislike it when you have such confidence in me."

"I know."

"You encourage my bad behaviour. My assertive side really does shine but people tend to hide from me when they know I'm on a mission. I'm pushy, Sophie. I won't take no for an answer."

"And that's what I love about you, Tony."

"I lose my coffee buddies during these times."

"I'll buy you all the coffees you want for a month if you get this done." Sophie bribed.

"Only a month, you say…" Thinking for a moment, Tony added, "Well, I suppose that will have to do. Just know that I will hold you to that."

"I'm sure you will, Tony." Sophie laughed.

"I'll get back to you." Tony was about to hang up, "And Sophie?"

"Yes?"

"I think it's wonderful you are supporting Omolara Orphanage and Adoption Agency."

"Thank you, Tony, but really, the person to thank would be Ethan Blackburn."

Hanging up from Tony, Sophie smiled. She adored Tony and often invited him and his partner, Jeff, over for dinner. She thought the world of the two of them. She thoroughly enjoyed her time with them, laughing and forgetting about the worries of the world.

The time seemed to drag on for Sophie as she waited to hear back from Tony until finally he called just after eight o'clock Thursday evening.

"Tony, tell me you got this done." Sophie was anxious to hear.

"Sophie, I deserve at least two months of coffee from you. I had to literally go to Brad Turner's home and interrupt his dinner party to get him to sign his approval of the motion. I was not very popular with Mrs. Turner, I might add. She actually threatened to haunt me after she dies…" Tony became momentarily quiet. "She's one scary lady."

Laughing, Sophie was waiting with baited breath. "I knew you could do it. You did get it done though, right?"

"I have now made enemies I never thought I could make but yes, I got it done."

Sophie screamed with delight.

"Tony, I wish I could kiss you right now. You are amazing. I'm giving you a raise when I get home."

"And the coffee, right?" Tony was relentless.

"And the coffee. Two month's worth." Sophie laughed. "Thank you, Tony. Now, go home and apologize to Jeff on my behalf for keeping you at work so late. I love you, Tony! You rock!"

"I can't help it, Sophie, it's just who I am." Tony hung up the phone and Sophie couldn't contain her happiness, jumping up and down with excitement. Saturday couldn't come soon enough.

TWENTY SEVEN

SOPHIE SPENT ALL DAY SATURDAY preparing. Having received the documentation and cheque by courier from Tony the day before, she prayed all day long that this would work out the way she had planned.

On Saturday evening she took one last look at herself in the mirror. She had to admit that she looked as good as she felt. She wore her new dress and heels, she went to a salon to have her hair done in an updo and she had her make-up applied to perfection. The dangly Swarovski crystal earrings she purchased and her mother's necklace completed the ensemble.

Smiling, she spritzed on some perfume and grabbed her bag.

She was going to a charity event.

Walking into the Mountainview Ballroom, Sophie was immediately offered a glass of champagne by a server dressed in a tuxedo. She was surprised at how many people were there. She estimated that there had to be a couple of hundred people at least. Looking around, the people she saw were dressed in gowns and tuxedos. She seemed to be the odd person out wearing a shorter dress but right now she didn't care nor did she have a choice.

She couldn't see Ethan anywhere, which actually worked out well for her. She wanted to keep a low profile until the right moment. Sophie wasn't sure what that moment would be or what she would do in that moment but decided she would know when it presented itself.

The room was decorated throughout with strings of shimmering lights. Banners were hung everywhere. Reading them, Sophie smiled. Omolara Orphanage and Adoption Agency. *You certainly can't miss these.* There was a live band playing soft music that gently flowed throughout the room as the muffled voices of the guests rose above it. She could hear the tinging of glasses as people exchanged empty flutes for ones filled with bubbling champagne. The aroma of the hors d'oeuvres being served smelled mouth-watering. As she walked past them, Sophie could smell the delicate scent of the multiple floral arrangements that were strategically placed throughout the room. She was in awe of how absolutely beautiful it was.

"Ms Callaghan, what a surprise to see you here."

Sophie turned to see Mrs. Cleverdon walking up to her.

"Mrs. Cleverdon, so nice to see you again." Sophie shook the older woman's hand. "You look wonderful."

"Well, thank you, my dear, and I must say the same of you. I've only ever seen you in a business setting at meetings back when I sat on the board. It's been a while. What brings you here tonight?"

"Supporting a friend." Sophie maintained discretion.

"Ah, yes, well, my husband and I are considering supporting this charity. We just aren't sure this is where our money should be directed. We shall make a decision this evening."

"Well, Mrs. Cleverdon, I think you would do well if you supported it. They are doing wonderful work. I know for a fact that Mr. Blackburn ensures all proceeds go directly to the charities he supports and his organization covers all administrative costs. It's a remarkable charity in Africa doing wonderful things for the children in their care. Mr. Blackburn personally ensures the funds are not misappropriated at any stage of the process. And more importantly, you would be helping the children who live there and the families who adopt them. You can't go wrong supporting them."

"That's lovely, thank you, Sophie. You are clearly a strong advocate of Mr. Blackburn's and this charity. That's rather reassuring coming from you. I'll be sure to speak to my husband but I can't see why he wouldn't be interested, given this information."

"That's wonderful to hear, Mrs. Cleverdon."

"Well, I must go and find my husband. You have a wonderful evening and by the way, I was very sorry to have heard about your mother and father. Both remarkable individuals. It was a pleasure working with them over the years. They are greatly missed."

"Thank you, Mrs. Cleverdon and you enjoy your evening as well." Sophie shook the woman's hand and smiled, happy to have had the opportunity to promote the orphanage. "Please be sure to say hello to your husband for me."

Within moments, there was a tinging of glasses which gained everyone's attention in the room. Soon after, someone called the guests to be seated so the true business of the evening could begin.

Sophie found an empty chair at a table at the back of the room. She wanted to remain out of Ethan's sight for now.

The first person to speak was Addison. Sophie rolled her eyes but also knew she wasn't in a position to judge given her previously poor behaviour.

Addison spoke highly of the orphanage. She spoke of how she and Ethan had spent countless hours at Omolara Orphanage getting acquainted with the director, employees, and the children.

Sitting listening to her speech, Sophie couldn't help but admit that Addison spoke very eloquently and could have anyone convinced to donate to their cause just from this speech alone.

Next came Ethan. Sophie's heart fluttered. She found it hard to focus on what he was saying. He looked so handsome in his tuxedo. Her mind wandered back to how she behaved when they last spoke with each other. She was clearly wrong and this was indeed an important event and charity.

After Ethan, several other individuals spoke about the benefits of supporting Omolara. The executive director of Omolara spoke, followed by some of the children who had previously been adopted from there. The children spoke of their wonderful experiences at the orphanage and how happy they were in their new homes which brought, not only Sophie to tears but as she observed, most everyone in the room.

The speeches were well done and the children who spoke were the icing on the cake. How could these people resist bidding?

After all of the speeches, it was announced that the live auction was about to begin. The auctioneer then stood up and explained that as they were aware, all the items being auctioned off were in the booklet handed to them as they walked in, including starting and incremental bids for each item.

This evening was not at all what she anticipated. When she decided to come to this event, she expected to just simply hand over her cheque as a company donation but she had to admit that she was finding it all rather intriguing.

Sophie looked around, found a booklet lying on the table and picked it up. She smiled as she read the inner cover and learned the meaning behind the name Omolara. 'Born at a perfect moment' or 'born at the right time'. Sophie loved the meaning.

Quickly scanning through the other pages, she discovered a wide variety of items such as trips, jewelry and even artwork done by some of the children. Placing it back on the table, it didn't matter to Sophie what was up on the auction block.

On the stage there was a large digital monitor with two numbers side by side. The auctioneer pointed out that the number on the right was the total amount they wanted to raise tonight. Twenty million dollars.

An ambitious undertaking.

The second number, which was currently at zero, would indicate the total amount of money progressively raised for the charity throughout the evening.

Sophie suspected if Mrs. Cleverdon was any example of the individuals in attendance, there was most assuredly a lot of money in this room. Individuals who, on a day-to-day basis, would be reluctant to easily give up their money but tonight, *should* give it up.

The first auction item came out… a painting done by one of the five year old orphans and framed by a famous artist who had hand carved the wood frame. Sophie acknowledged that this painting was clearly done by a five-year-old and certainly not worth the money they were about to spend but that wouldn't matter to the people bidding because the frame itself was, in fact, the art and they were essentially donating their money with the added bonus of receiving a picture framed by a famous artist who had signed and numbered the piece. It would be a one-of-a-kind piece they could show their friends.

The bidding started at ten thousand dollars and went up by increments of five thousand. One individual tried to place an incremental bid of twenty-five hundred dollars and the auctioneer poked fun suggesting he needed to open his pockets a little wider, to the amusement of all the guests. As each guest placed a bid, they raised a placard with their company or individual name for the auctioneer who eventually announced the names of the winners for the recorder to keep track on a laptop computer.

It didn't take long for the progressive total to reach close to one million dollars after just a few items. Sophie was impressed.

"Sold! Fifty thousand dollars from Alexander Davidson of Gibbons and Davidson Financials. Thank you, Alex. I'm sure you will enjoy that weekend away. That brings the total amount raised to seven hundred and fifty thousand dollars."

"Now up, is this wonderful sculpture."

Sophie listened as the auctioneer described the sculpture and who the artist was before beginning the bidding.

"Can I get a starting bid of ten thousand dollars?"

The auctioneer worked the room, easily increasing the bidding on the sculpture. Soon Sophie saw a placard rise up not far from where she was sitting.

"Thank you very much. We now have a sixty thousand dollar bid for this beautiful sculpture. Do I hear seventy thousand? Anyone?" Looking around the room the auctioneer waited.

"Okay then, that's sixty thousand dollars going once. Sixty thousand dollars going twice. Sold! That's sixty thousand dollars from Richard Cleverdon of RSC Construction for this stunning piece of art. Thanks Richard, I'm glad to see you were feeling generous tonight."

She did it. Mrs. Cleverdon had convinced her husband this was a good cause. Sophie was pleased that their conversation had made a difference.

And so the auctioneer carried on, with the odd moment of joking with the guests, keeping the event light and entertaining. He clearly knew these people, knew how to work a room, and exactly what to do to generate bids. He was good at his job.

Throughout the bidding, Sophie watched as Ethan and Addison periodically walked off stage then back on again smiling and laughing as they conversed with various people. Her jealousy nerve twitched a little but she kept it at bay understanding what was actually going on here.

The number on the monitor kept creeping closer to the twenty million that was hoped for.

"We have now raised a total of thirteen million dollars, folks. Only another seven million to go. Don't shut your wallets just yet."

As the evening went along, with each item being sold, Sophie was amazed at how generous people were.

The auctioneer continued working his way through the items left to sell.

"Do I hear ten thousand dollars more for this beautiful diamond necklace?"

A placard rose up from a table in the middle of the room.

"Thank you Gretchen Halliday of Halliday Mercedes for your bid of seventy five thousand dollars. Did your husband buy that for you or for his girlfriend?" Charlie nodded then winked at Gretchen's husband sitting beside her.

"I bought it for myself." Gretchen shouted back. A roar of laughter followed as Gretchen and her husband laughed along with the crowd.

Throughout the evening the bidding had gone very quickly and the money raised was now within reach of their twenty million dollar goal but they were on their last auction item and falling short. By now the bidding had slowed up significantly. It was looking like they weren't going to make their goal.

"This is a very expensive cruise being offered on a private yacht with personal staff and it even has its own helipad and helicopter. It's all expenses paid for a month in the Mediterranean. It can't get any better than this. We have a bid of two hundred and fifty thousand dollars. Can I get five hundred thousand?"

Before continuing, Charlie added, "Remember, ladies and gentlemen, we need another six million five hundred thousand to reach our goal and we are down to our last item. Surely someone must be able to step up and place another bid on this spectacular cruise which, by the way, includes flights for up to four individuals."

Within moments a placard raised up from one side of the room.

"Thank you for your bid of five hundred thousand dollars, Jane Bottoms of Bottoms Up Vineyards."

"Ladies and gentlemen, do I hear one million dollars?" Charlie waited patiently. "Someone must be in need of a vacation. I know I will be after this night is over."

Laughter was heard throughout the room.

Within moments, from the back of the room, another placard popped up drawing a smile from Charlie. His pleas seemed to bring new life to the bidding.

"Thank you Lexi Morris of Greene Financials for your bid of one million dollars. Can I get one million five hundred thousand?"

With that, another placard towards the front of the room raised up and someone shouted, "Two million five hundred thousand."

Charlie smiled.

"Wonderful! Thank you, Joan! I have a bid of two million five hundred thousand dollars from Joan Navarro of Point Line Computers. That brings us to our last four million dollars folks. Can I get another bid for this spectacular trip?"

Suddenly the bidding halted and the room grew quiet.

"Any one at all? Jane?"

Jane shook her head no.

"You're making me work for my paycheque, folks, but if I don't raise this money I'm going to get fired." Charlie was putting the pressure on.

People quietly chuckled but no one would bid.

Looking over the crowd, Charlie spotted someone.

"Surely, Martin Thorold, if you can afford that expensive car you're driving, you can bid on this trip."

"Charlie, I'm tapped out."

"Well, okay Martin, I'm sorry to hear that. I might have a part time job for you at the auction house." Martin laughed at the joke along with the crowd.

Looking around the room, Charlie caught sight of someone else.

"George, what about you? You certainly don't need to invest in another expensive suit from Brown's."

"Sorry, Charlie."

"Well, alright then, folks. We have a bid of two million five hundred thousand dollars. Going once..." Charlie waited.

"Going twice..." Charlie took a moment to scan the room.

"Sold for two million five hundred thousand dollars to Joan Navarro of Point Line Computers! Thank you, Joan. I'm sure you, Ken and the kids will enjoy the time away."

"So, ladies and gentlemen, here's my dilemma." Charlie grabbed the microphone and walked across the stage as he spoke.

"We no longer have any items to auction off and we still have four million dollars to raise. I've been commissioned to raise twenty million dollars for this wonderful charity and the children of Omolara Orphanage." Walking to the middle of the stage, Charlie continued.

"Those of you who know me, know very well that I'm not leaving here tonight until that money has been raised. It's highly unusual, however, I'm left with no other option than to ask that the last four million dollars be straight up donated for this very worthy cause."

Charlie was a well respected auctioneer throughout the area and the audience was listening intently as he spoke.

"So, we are going to get this started by opening the bidding up at fifty thousand dollars."

The room grew uncomfortably quiet as people sipped on their drinks and waited.

"Fifty thousand dollars." Charlie called out again. "Do I hear fifty thousand dollars?"

Sophie looked around to see most everyone shaking their heads, quietly speaking amongst themselves then looking from side to side to see if anyone would come forward.

Charlie scanned the now very quiet room.

"How about forty thousand? Can I hear forty thousand dollars to help the children of Omolara Orphanage?"

Still no one came forward with a bid. It was becoming apparent that they were going to fall short of their goal.

Sophie sighed. *Okay then.* She had wanted to do this quietly but decided this was the moment she was waiting on.

She didn't have a placard so, standing up, Sophie shouted from the back of the room, to the auctioneer.

"Two million dollars!"

Everyone turned to look at her and the auctioneer broke into a big smile.

"Two million dollars! Thank you! Two million dollars has been bid from…" Stopping, he addressed Sophie. "What is your name and organization, Miss?"

Sophie could see Ethan looking in her direction suddenly recognizing it was her. At first she couldn't speak as their eyes locked.

"Miss, what is your name and organization?" Charlie called out once again.

Looking over to the auctioneer, Sophie shouted, "Sophie Callaghan of Callaghan Hotels."

Looking over at Ethan, she saw the shocked look on his face. She saw Addison looking at her and then back at Ethan. She saw people from the other tables staring back at her. She suddenly felt uncomfortable with the attention. Time seemed to stand still but within moments, the room resonated with the sound of applause. Sophie sat back down again.

Charlie shouted, "Two million dollars from Sophie Callaghan of Callaghan Hotels. Can I hear two more million dollars so we can meet this goal, wrap this night up and I don't have to harass you kind people any further?" Laughter erupted.

Within moments, Sophie watched as Ethan stood up and walked over to the microphone where Charlie stood. Charlie stepped aside and Ethan spoke, looking directly at Sophie.

"If Callaghan Hotels can make a two million dollar donation then far be it for Tuxedo Hotels not to match it." Smiling in Sophie's direction, Ethan shouted, "Two million dollars from Ethan Blackburn of Tuxedo Hotels."

Ethan stepped away from the microphone allowing Charlie to take his place.

"Thank you very much, Ethan. That would be two million dollars from Ethan Blackburn of Tuxedo Hotels." Charlie looked back at Ethan and nodded.

"And we have achieved our goal of twenty million dollars, folks. Thank you very much for your generosity and for supporting Omolara Orphanage and Adoption Agency. The auction has now ended."

The place erupted with cheering and clapping.

"Be sure to settle up with the cashier by the door before you leave this evening." Charlie announced. Shaking hands with Ethan, Addison, and the executive director of Omolara, Charlie waved good-bye to the guests before leaving the stage.

The crowd began to disperse and Sophie left, quickly dropping off her cheque with the cashier on her way out the door. She didn't want to speak to Ethan right now. It was too complicated and could become too emotional for her and besides it wasn't the night to make this about her.

Hopping into a taxi, Sophie headed back to the hotel. She'd done what she came to do and it couldn't have turned out better. She needed to be sure to give Tony a big hug when she returned to the office. If not for him, this wouldn't have been possible.

"Oh, I can't wait to tell Anika what happened. That was one of the most exciting moments of my life."

Arriving back in her suite, Sophie reminisced about the evening as she changed into casual clothes and pulled her hair down.

Mom, you would have been so proud. I feel so damn good right now. Sophie couldn't stop smiling. She was far from tired regardless of the late hour.

Hungry, Sophie knew the restaurant would be closed and went to the coffee shop to get a drink and sandwich. Sitting by herself at one of the small tables, she still felt euphoric. If it worked out with Ethan, she would be thrilled but if it didn't, then she had helped a wonderful charity and some kids who needed it. It was win-win for her either direction it went.

Finishing up her sandwich, she was surprised to see Anika out in the lobby at such a late hour but then remembered the students coming the next day. Calling out to her, Anika smiled and joined her for a coffee at the table.

Telling Anika all about what took place, Anika beamed. Sophie, I'm so proud of you. I knew you would figure this all out. Your parents would be very proud."

"Anika, it was the best feeling in the world. It was so excit…"

Sophie stopped talking. Seeing her looking out to the lobby, Anika turned to see what she was looking at and nodded.

"Well, I think I should be going. You have a lovely evening and again, I'm very proud of you, Sophie." Walking away, Anika nodded at Ethan as she walked past him.

Sophie stood and walked out to him but couldn't speak. She wasn't sure what direction the conversation would go, especially now he knew who she was.

"Why didn't you tell me you were a Callaghan?"

"I should have." Sophie waited before asking, "Would it have made a difference?" She was nervous.

Ethan said nothing, pondering her question.

Suddenly he scooped her up in his arms, lifted her off the floor and kissed her. She was relieved beyond words. She had hoped he would forgive her.

Putting her back down again, Sophie spoke quickly.

"Ethan, I'm so sorry with the way I behaved…"

"Sophie, let's go upstairs."

TWENTY EIGHT

SOPHIE WAS CONTENT LYING NAKED with Ethan's muscular arms wrapped around her, his naked body warm and strong beside her. She had never had a better day in her life and it was one that would be difficult to repeat.

Her body tingled feeling him kiss her on the back of the neck. As his hands slowly made their way to her breasts, Sophie was responsive to his touch as he caressed her nipples gently with his fingers.

Turning onto her back, Ethan slowly slid inside of her as they made love once more.

The next morning Sophie showered and dressed then sat in the living room waiting for Ethan to join her. She knew they needed to talk. Not so much about their argument but about the fact that she had finally revealed who she was.

Walking out of the bedroom, Ethan stopped and smiled at Sophie.

"So, I think we have some catching up to do."

"Agreed." Sophie felt awkward to be discussing who she was given so much time had passed since they first met.

"When I thought about it, I realized you had never mentioned your last name to me and I never thought to ask. Do you realize what a shock last night was for me? In a good way, mind you."

"By the time I found out who your father was, I just couldn't fess up, especially after what you had said at the hospital that night. I didn't want you thinking I was a…"

"Gold-digger." Ethan acknowledged.

"Well no." Sophie felt awkward trying to explain her position. "I didn't want you thinking I was trying to get inside information. Then as time went by, I really liked you and our relationship grew and well…I just didn't know how to tell you or even whether I should tell you."

"Fair enough." Ethan understood. "Clearly not a gold-digger."

"Not a gold-digger." Sophie grinned. "Although, competitor could be an issue…"

"I think we need to just put that in the back of our minds. I'm content making our relationship the focus for now." Ethan reassured Sophie.

Sophie nodded.

"Listen Ethan, please forgive me for my horrible behaviour last week. It was completely uncalled for and I was wrong. I should have been more understanding. I'm sorry. It really was an important charity and event. I should have listened and not been so closed minded about your situation with Addison."

"Well, I wasn't exactly on my best behaviour either, so perhaps we could call it even."

"Deal." Sophie was relieved.

"I must say, you had an awful lot of people talking about what you did last night. To say it ended a wonderful evening on a very dramatic note is an understatement. It was a very generous donation. I can't thank you enough."

"It was a pleasure to be able to help such a wonderful cause."

"Well, to say it is going to greatly help the kids and staff is understating the obvious." Reflecting back on the evening, Ethan was having difficulty reining in his emotions, which was not typical of him.

"That was an ambitious achievement. I'm impressed and I am even just a little bit reluctant to admit that Addison is quite an impressive speaker. No one could possibly refuse donating to anything she asked for. I see why you work with her. She seems to get it done."

"That she does. She is remarkable and shines in situations like this. It's her forte."

"I'm just glad I could be a small part of it."

"I would suggest that two million dollars is no small part." Laughing, Ethan then added, "If you would like, I could take you for a tour of the office here, learn more about it. I think you would be impressed with what they have accomplished given their lack of resources. Now, thanks to donors such as yourself and everyone last night, they can achieve whatever they need to, whether it's improving building structure, updating accommodations for the children, buying them the personal things they need...even giving them a Christmas, which was a stretch in the past. This fundraiser will keep them running for many years to come. This has been several years in the making and I can't tell you how relieved I am that it was such a success."

"You should be very proud."

Sophie smiled warmly watching Ethan speak of the orphanage. She had never seen him this excited about anything, not that she had known him long but from what she had seen of him, it was obvious this was something he was passionate about.

"Well, I'd better get going. I have to wrap a few things up today at the banquet hall and settle up with Charlie. Are you free tomorrow for dinner?"

"Yes, I believe I am."

Giving Sophie a warm hug and kiss, Ethan left Sophie alone contemplating how her week had been such an emotional roller-coaster.

Now if I can ever get this estate of mother's wrapped up. This is their last week to sign off and I can't wait. God knows what will happen after that. I just don't even want to think about it. I'll deal with it as it comes. Maybe they won't even sign.

Sophie spent the day going over emails that Tony had sent her.

I can't wait to call and tell Tony all about what happened. I know he will be thrilled.

By late afternoon Sophie was exhausted. Housekeeping had come and gone and she decided she needed to take a nap. She hadn't slept much the night before, which she certainly wasn't complaining about. Her time with Ethan had been beyond wonderful but she needed to sleep. She couldn't stay up all night like she once could.

Crawling into the freshly made bed, Sophie took in a deep breath of the clean sheets and sighed contentedly before falling into a deep sleep.

Waking up, Sophie stretched and opened her eyes to bright sunshine warmly lighting up the room.

I mustn't have slept long. It's still daylight out but I surprisingly feel rested. Checking her phone, she was shocked to realize she had slept through the night. She had clearly been more tired than she thought.

Jumping out of bed she got dressed and called Tony, telling him all about the event.

TWENTY NINE

MONDAY NIGHT ARRIVED AND SOPHIE had arranged to meet Ethan in the hotel restaurant for dinner.

Ethan arrived shortly after Sophie sat down, pleased to see his favourite red wine on the table.

"I didn't think you would mind having dinner at the competition's restaurant." Sophie mischievously grinned.

"Not at all." Ethan laughed.

"Did you get everything settled at the banquet hall?"

"Yes, we still have items that will require delivery, however, that's all been arranged and they should arrive this week at the respective homes or businesses. As far as Charlie is concerned, he was paid yesterday and once the funds are compiled they will be transferred to Omolara as soon their chief financial officer is prepared to receive them. There are processes to be followed but it will all be taken care of within the next couple of weeks."

"That's fantastic." Taking a sip of wine, Sophie had to ask, "Have you told your dad about us?" Sophie wondered how Winston reacted after the news.

"No, I haven't seen Dad in a few days. I've been too busy with the auction. I won't see him now for a day or two. He said he was going to our cabin in the mountains and will be home on Thursday. I'm sure when he returns he will want to have you in for dinner again. We can tell him together at that time."

"Perhaps you should speak to him privately before he sees me. You just don't know how he might react." Sophie was concerned.

"I can assure you that all will be fine, Sophie. He really likes you."

"And Addison?" Sophie was hesitant to bring her up but needed to know.

"What about Addison?"

"Was she upset that I was there?"

"Shocked is a better word. More about who you are than about your being there, not to mention, the money you donated and in such a dramatic fashion."

Sophie nodded with understanding.

"She is not too happy with me, though."

"Oh? And why is that?"

"She thought that because I was there that night under the guise that all was well, that we were 'engaged' again. I had to make it perfectly clear that we were not and that we were only allowing people to think nothing had changed between us for the sake of the event that night."

"I'm sure that wouldn't have gone over very well." Sophie almost felt sorry for Addison.

"She told me I could go to hell and take my second class girlfriend with me."

"Oh." Sophie was taken aback by the reference but understood Addison would have been hurt and angry.

"Then, when she found out who you were, well, that just about put her over the edge. She wasn't quite sure what to say. On one hand she doesn't like you..."

"Well, thank you for that."

"...and on the other hand, you made a significant contribution to a charity she's passionate about."

Sophie nodded with understanding. Thinking for a moment, she asked, "Why so passionate?" She was curious.

"Well, Addison was herself adopted as a young girl from a Russian orphanage and when I brought the idea to her of supporting Omolara, let's just say, there was no holding her back. Her experience hadn't been quite as kind to her as Omolara has been to the children in their care. Addison really just wanted to be a part of something that was near and dear to her heart. She has especially given much time, energy and passion to ensuring this event in particular was successful."

"Very commendable." Sophie hated to admit that a small part of her admired Addison's passion.

Ethan continued, "Anyway, it's hard to be angry with someone who has, in her opinion, 'status in the community' and who helped her particular cause so significantly."

"Ah, I see."

"So, she decided to be angry with me instead, broke off our engagement and said she never wanted to see me again."

"But you really weren't engaged...and, you broke up with her before." Sophie was a little confused by it all.

"Ah, yes, but as far as Addison is concerned, we were engaged, we broke up, we got back together again that night and now she broke it off. I think she just wanted to be able to save face when the media gets hold of the news. That way she can say she ended it."

"And how are you feeling about all of this? I know you were concerned about people losing confidence in you both…"

"That is true." Ethan felt slightly awkward about making such a nonsensical statement that night. "It's fine. I was worried about nothing."

"Are you ready to order, Ms Callaghan?"

"I'm sorry, Marvin, we have been so busy talking we haven't made a decision."

"I'll return shortly." Nodding to both Sophie and Ethan, Marvin topped up their wine and quickly moved on to the next table.

"What do you recommend?" Ethan scanned the menu.

"Well, admittedly, you were right about the beef Wellington. It was delicious."

"It's a specialty of the chef here. You can't go wrong ordering it." Sophie smiled, pleased that Ethan's first meal here was a good one.

"Well, I must be off. I have an early day tomorrow." Finishing his wine, Ethan asked, "I meant to ask you, did you ever get that family business sorted out that you came here for?"

"It should be wrapped up by the end of next week, and…by wrapped up I mean, I'm hoping to at least pass along the information I have for them."

"Well, I hope everything works out."

"Did you want to get dinner tomorrow night?" Sophie couldn't wait to see him again.

"Wish I could but I made a promise to someone that I really need to keep. How about Wednesday?"

"Okay, sure."

"It's a date!"

Walking Ethan to the hotel entrance, Sophie leaned in and kissed him good-bye.

THIRTY

THE NEXT DAY, SOPHIE DECIDED to take a drive and get reacquainted with Granite Hill. It had been a long time since she had been here last and there had been significant changes. Driving through the busy downtown core and towards the outskirts of the city she was amazed at how much it had grown. Housing had developed extensively. New industry, although confined to an area north of the city, was clearly booming.

Granite Hill had traditionally been known for its mining, logging and forestry but tourism had quickly become one of the top industries for the area. She could understand that, given its stunning location near the mountains and the ocean not far away. Ski hills popped up making winter prime time for tourism and to top it all off, Granite Hill became a sought after area for the film industry.

Driving up through the mountains, Sophie was gone for several hours enjoying the scenery before deciding to return to the city.

By late afternoon she decided to head back to the hotel but somehow managed to get lost and had a difficult time finding her way back. Finally, pulling over, she started to put the hotel address into the GPS when she happened to look up and saw a directional sign for the Omolara Orphanage and Adoption Agency. Curiosity got the better of her and she decided to drive by.

Following the signs, Sophie pulled up and parked on the street in front of a rather small five-storey red brick building that looked like an industrial office building.

I'll definitely have to get Ethan to take me on a tour…

Looking across the courtyard, Sophie was surprised to see Ethan pull up in the parking lot and wait in his car. Shortly thereafter, another car pulled up and she saw a rather attractive woman get out and greet him with a hug and a kiss on the cheek before they both got into her car and drove away.

"What the heck?"

Sophie wondered what was going on and decided to follow the car. They drove several kilometres then pulled into a parking lot and parked. She watched as they walked across the street into Café de Phil. Sophie wanted to know who this woman was that Ethan was with. She wasn't jealous…or so she told herself. She was just…curious.

Parking, Sophie got out of her car and walked over to the coffee shop. She tried to peek into the front window to catch a glimpse of Ethan and the woman but there was a curtain hung on the lower half of the window and it was in her line of vision. Grabbing a patio chair, she pulled it over to the window. Stepping up, she crouched on the chair, peeked through the window and looked around the coffee shop until she finally found Ethan and the woman trying to decide where to sit. They decided to sit at a table towards the middle of the room. Sophie watched as they placed their order with the server then began talking. She wondered why they were being so secretive, first meeting at Omolara and then driving to the café in her car. It seemed so…

Yikes! I hope he didn't see me. My God! He looked towards the window, I think, right at me.

Waiting for a minute, Sophie slowly pulled herself back up again and peeked in, this time, Ethan wasn't there. Looking all over the restaurant, she couldn't see him anywhere, only the woman.

"Maybe he went to the washroom." She quietly spoke to herself.

"Or, maybe he's right behind you."

Screaming, Sophie fell off the chair and onto the ground hitting her head on the table as she went and landing hard on her butt.

"Ow!" She wasn't sure whether to hold her head or her butt, both hurt enough to require attention.

Ethan helped her up then stood staring at her with the look of a parent when their kids are caught doing something they shouldn't. Sophie felt as guilty as one of those kids.

"What are you doing?"

"Um...well..."

"It looks like you're spying on me or is there someone else in this restaurant you know?" Ethan peeked in the window, looked around then stood back with his arms crossed. Sophie knew she had some explaining to do.

"No, I..." She frantically wracked her brain for a response. "You see..."

"I'm listening..." Ethan waited patiently.

"I needed a coffee." Sophie lied.

"Really?"

"Yeah."

"Here, at this particular coffee shop so far away from your hotel that actually has a coffee shop in it?" Ethan knew she was lying.

"Yup." Sophie couldn't look him in the eyes. She was a terrible liar - she knew it.

"Crouching on a patio chair..."

"Yeah." Sophie nodded like the guilty person she was.

"Peeking into the window..."

"Well, I wondered where my server was." Sophie was digging the hole deeper with every word she spoke.

"Spying on me…" Ethan nailed it home.

"Yup!"

Sophie suddenly realized that she had inadvertently confessed.

"I mean, no, of course not!"

"Okay, the game is up, Sophie. Why are you spying on me?" Ethan's tone was firm and Sophie knew it was over.

Hanging her head, she was utterly embarrassed by her behaviour.

"Oh my God, Ethan. I'm sorry. I really hadn't intended to do this. It was a total coincidence that I came across you. I got lost and saw a sign for the orphanage so I drove there to see what it looked like. That's when I saw you pulling into the parking lot."

"Ah, I see and then you saw a woman pull in and we drove away together." Ethan was understanding much clearer than Sophie had hoped.

"Well, yes…" Sophie scrunched up her face, horrified that Ethan had caught her in such a compromising position.

"Okay then. Would you like to come in and meet the woman I skulked off with?"

"No…I mean, sure." Sophie cringed. *Oh my God! Could this day get anymore humiliating? I think not.*

Following Ethan into the coffee shop, they walked over to the table where the woman he 'skulked off' with was sitting patiently sipping on her drink.

Looking up, she broke into a big smile seeing them approach.

"Lucy, I'd like you to meet Sophie. Sophie, this is Lucy."

"Hello Sophie! So nice to meet you. Ethan has told me so much about you."

Sophie looked at Ethan who in turn gave her a knowing look.

"Yes, Sophie, I've told Lucy all about you." Ethan's mocking just added to her humiliation.

"Nice to meet you, Lucy." Sophie shook Lucy's hand. Feeling completely uncomfortable, she decided it was time to leave before she made things worse. "Well, I had better go now and let you both finish up here."

"Please don't leave on my account." Lucy smiled. "I'm fine with Sophie being here, Ethan."

"Well, there you go, Sophie, you can actually have a coffee in here with us instead of out on the patio."

Sophie gave him an irritated look in return.

Laughing, Ethan offered, "What would you like to drink? I'll get it for you."

"A shot of whiskey..." she answered truthfully. "However, I'll have a cappuccino." Sitting down, Sophie wasn't sure what to say to Lucy.

"So, Ethan and I are discussing the possibility of my partner and I adopting from Omolara. We've been unsuccessful trying to adopt from other agencies."

"That's wonderful but I'm sorry you haven't been able to adopt through other agencies." Sophie grew very interested in the conversation.

"Ah, yes, well when you are gay it creates a bit of a problem."

"Oh, I see." Sophie felt even more humiliated by her unwarranted snooping around. "Truthfully, I don't see. Why would being gay be an issue? I just can't see that it should be."

"I agree and my partner agrees but unfortunately we've had difficulty convincing other agencies, all of which have very strict adoption policies. So that's where Ethan has been helping us."

"Really? How is he helping?"

"Here you go." Ethan placed Sophie's drink down in front of her.

"I hear you are helping Lucy and her partner adopt."

"Yes, that's right. Addison and I sit on the board of directors for the North American office and we have set some very specific policies that don't allow this type of discrimination to take place. This will be an agency that allows adoptions to take place for all couples regardless of their sexual orientation. As long as they go through the screening process and are deemed a safe, loving home for a child then they shall be allowed to adopt through our agency. It just recently passed with the board of directors and I wanted to let Lucy know in person."

"That's wonderful. Lucy, I'm so happy for you. This shouldn't have been an issue to begin with, but I'm so glad it really isn't now with Omolara." Sophie was genuinely excited for Lucy and her partner.

"Thank you so much. Tanya and I are really very excited to start the process and thanks to Ethan and Addison, we can."

"We wanted our policies to reflect the direction our agency is heading." Ethan reassured her.

"The issue for us, Sophie, was entirely that we were a gay couple wanting to adopt."

"Well, I'm happy it's going to work out for you both. Sounds like you have all done some fantastic work." Sophie was genuinely happy for Lucy and Tanya.

"Lucy, Sophie here was one of our biggest financial contributors and one of the main reasons we were able to reach our fundraising goal last weekend."

"So, I should be saying, thank you." Lucy smiled.

"No thanks necessary. It's a pleasure to help such a wonderful organization." Sophie was sincere about her feelings.

"Well, Ethan, I should get going. I told Tanya I would pick her up. Sophie, it was wonderful to meet you and I hope we see each other again."

"It was a pleasure meeting you as well. Good luck with the adoption." Sophie really liked Lucy.

"Do you need me to take you back to your car, Ethan?"

"No, I'm sure I can get a ride with Sophie."

"Thanks for everything, Ethan, and please thank Addison for us as well." Lucy walked over and gave Ethan a hug and kiss on the cheek.

"Let me know if you need anything else." Ethan offered.

"I will, and thanks again."

After Lucy left, Sophie's awkwardness was evident.

"Ethan…"

"Oh, don't bother saying a word. I'm sure there is nothing you could say to redeem yourself right about now so let's just move on. You've already humiliated yourself…rather well I might add, so I figure that's punishment enough." Ethan admonished Sophie.

"To say the least," she mumbled.

"So, I'm free now. Did you want to go for dinner?"

"I thought you had someplace to be tonight?"

"Normally, I would have an Omolara board meeting but it was cancelled so I arranged to meet with Lucy instead to give her the good news in person. Next month is the meeting I really must attend because we are going to be discussing the building of an elementary school within the orphanage for the children who live there."

"That's fantastic, Ethan! Where do the children go for school right now?"

"They have to be walked approximately ten kilometres to school and it's too far for any of the children, let alone the younger kids, especially given the high temperatures there. Anyway, we had discussed building a school at a later date, however, the directors from the orphanage requested it be built sooner than later with some of the proceeds from the fundraiser going towards that project. We will need to do other fundraisers but for now we have enough to get started."

Sophie could hear the excitement in Ethan's voice. The smile on his face when he spoke was heartwarming. He was genuinely excited about this. It didn't seem to be just another charity to him.

THIRTY ONE

THE DAYS DRAGGED ON FOR Sophie, who was anxious to get her mother's estate finalized once and for all. On Wednesday of the following week, she lay in bed just staring out the window, watching the rain fall. Finally dragging herself out of bed, she showered and dressed. She was about to go downstairs for breakfast when her phone rang. Picking it up, she was relieved to hear that it was Mr. Hawthorne.

"Ms Callaghan, I have some good news."

"Thank goodness."

"My client has agreed to meet tomorrow but will not be able to finalize things until Friday."

"What? But, why can't it be finalized tomorrow, Mr. Hawthorne?" Sophie grew angry. "This has gone on long enough."

"Please hear me out."

Sophie sighed, "Very well, please go on."

"They would like to meet initially to hear what you have to say and how it may or may not affect their family, then, if necessary, discuss it with their family and finalize things Friday afternoon."

"This really is getting to be too much, Mr. Hawthorne. I just don't understand the reasoning behind this drawn out and complicated response."

"I expect my client will be happy to explain at the meeting tomorrow, if you are in agreement." Mr. Hawthorne seemed to be an individual who didn't get too overly concerned about much of anything and Sophie found it frustrating, although, she suspected that helped him in his role as a lawyer.

Thinking on what Mr. Hawthorne said, Sophie really had no choice but to agree to the request.

"Very well. What time tomorrow can we meet?"

"Wonderful, Let's meet at one o'clock at my office here on Spring Lake Boulevard."

"I'll see you then."

Sophie hung up the phone. *This client of his is going to get an earful from me when we meet. This has been a ridiculous roundabout way to accomplish something so simple. All they had to do was come in, review everything and sign the damn papers. How fucking difficult is that? Mother, you are not in my good books right now.*

Thursday arrived and Sophie was actually quite nervous about this meeting. She wasn't sure what to expect and she was positive the other party certainly didn't.

Dressing in the only power suit that she brought with her, Sophie checked one last time in the mirror before heading out to Mr. Hawthorne's office.

Walking into the very impressive looking office building, Sophie noticed how quiet it was even though there were many people milling about going from place to place. It was a large reception area filled with leather easy chairs, marble floors and an oversized reception desk which sat under the rather large sign reading Maison, McIlroy and Hawthorne on the wall behind. Sitting behind the desk was a young man who looked like he was barely out of high school yet looked extremely professional, dressed in his navy blue business suit.

Sophie walked up to the desk.

"I'm here to see…" She was stopped cold by an index finger popping up in front of her.

"Mr. Maison is currently out of the office. I'll put you through to his assistant, Carol. One moment please."

Sophie hadn't even heard a phone ring and quickly realized that there had been no ring.

"Maison, McIlroy and Hawthorne, how may I help you?"

"One moment please."

"Maison, McIlroy and Hawthorne, how may I help you?"

"Yes, of course, I'll put you right through to Mr. Sanchez. One moment please."

Sophie waited patiently for several more calls before the young man finally directed his attention to her.

"Who are you here to see?"

"Mr. Hawthorne."

"Your name please?"

"Sophie Callaghan."

"You may take a seat and I'll let Mr. Hawthorne know you are here to see him."

It didn't take long for someone to greet Sophie.

"Ms Callaghan."

"Yes." Standing, Sophie found herself facing a young, rather handsome man who seemed to be in his late twenties, if she were to guess.

"I'm Richard. Mr. Hawthorne's assistant. I'll take you in."

Following Richard through the large glass doors, they continued down a very long carpeted hallway that was a combination of beautiful artwork and office doors. Richard then guided her into an enormous board room with a large rectangular shaped wooden table in the middle and without counting, Sophie estimated approximately two dozen chairs carefully placed around it.

"Please have a seat. Can I get you something to drink?"

"No, thank you."

"Very well. Mr. Hawthorne will be with you shortly."

Sophie faced a very large window which looked out over the city and the multitude of high-rises that was the Granite Hill business district. Opening her briefcase, Sophie pulled out the papers that she required signing as well as a copy of her mother's will and other documentation that she expected Mr. Hawthorne's client would request to see. Anything else Sophie could arrange for Tony to send at a later date. Placing everything neatly on the table, it wasn't long before she heard the boardroom door open.

"Sophie! So wonderful to finally meet you." Mr. Hawthorne was a tall man with a husky build, balding and a very warm smile that relaxed Sophie immediately.

Sophie stood up. "Mr. Hawthorne. So nice to meet you as well."

"Please be seated. My client has arrived and Richard will show them in shortly. Just a reminder that they have come to review everything with you but would like another meeting tomorrow to sign everything off if that is the outcome. Today is more to understand exactly what is about to take place. I thought you would like to go over everything with them. I only provided the basics. In fact, I didn't even give them your name or tell them who they were meeting with. They assume they are meeting with your mother's lawyer. I thought it best not to divulge this information until you officially met, for your privacy."

"That's fine, thank you, Mr. Hawthorne. I must admit, I'm rather nervous about everything and about meeting your client, as I expect they will be as well. They must have been completely shocked to hear…"

Just then there was a knock at the door.

"Come in, Richard." Mr. Hawthorne stood and walked over to the door.

Sophie stood and turned around just as Mr. Hawthorne's client entered the room and immediately fell back down into her seat again.

Oh my God!

THIRTY TWO

Sophie was dumbstruck. She couldn't find the words.

"Sophie?"

"Winston? I don't understand." Sophie's mind was racing trying to put the pieces together in her mind.

"You two know each other?" Mr. Hawthorne was just as confused as they were.

"We do, yes." Winston answered.

"Well, please sit down."

Winston found a seat and they all sat down, quietly confused by what was going on.

"Winston…" Sophie was taken aback and didn't know where to begin. "Did you know my mother?"

Nodding, Winston smiled. "I did, yes, very well. And your father."

Sophie's mouth dropped open. She suddenly felt emotional and tears came to her eyes.

"Sophie, I wasn't aware that you were Sophie Callaghan. Why did you never say anything?"

"It just never came up, Winston, and then when I was visiting you and you mentioned you owned Tuxedo Hotels, I wasn't sure what to say. I didn't want you thinking I was befriending you for inside information."

"I would never have thought that, my dear, but I do understand your dilemma." Winston sat thinking for a moment. "This does put a whole new light on things, I must admit."

"I'm sorry, I should have said something." Sophie now realized that saying nothing was creating a new set of concerns that she hadn't anticipated.

"Marcel, could you please give us some privacy. I think we have a few things to discuss before we get to the legal matters that we are here for."

"Of course, Winston. Take as long as you need. I have the board room booked for the next four hours." Mr. Hawthorne quietly got up to leave and shut the door behind him.

"Winston, how did you know my parents? I don't understand what's going on right now."

Winston took in a deep breath and sighed quietly before speaking.

"You see Sophie, it was all a very long time ago. Your mother, father and I were once very good friends. We were together all the time. We knew each other from our high school days and then we all went to university together. We really were inseparable."

"I don't remember my parents ever speaking of you, though."

"Ah yes, understandable. Please let me continue."

Sophie nodded, eager to hear more.

"You see, after university your parents and I went into business together. As a matter of fact, we opened up a hotel together. Well, over time, we planned to open more hotels. However, something unfortunate happened that ended our partnership for good."

"Which was?" Sophie wanted desperately to understand.

"I hesitate to continue for fear of hurting you, my dear."

"Winston, there couldn't possibly be any surprises that could shock me more than what my mother already disclosed during the reading of her will."

"And please let me say how sorry I was to hear of your mother and father's accident. It devastated me. Regardless of our past, I still loved them both dearly."

Sophie nodded.

"Well, let me continue. Our partnership ended because your mother and I had an affair."

Sophie's eyes grew large. *I was wrong. I can be shocked.*

"You and my mother…"

"Yes."

"Was this after my parents were married?"

"No, it was before, however, they were engaged to be married."

"I see."

"And she became pregnant…" Winston cautiously proceeded.

"With your baby…" The pieces of the puzzle were starting to fall into place.

Winston closed his eyes and took a moment. Opening them again he nodded.

"Yes."

All of a sudden the reality of what was just divulged hit her and Sophie immediately panicked.

"Oh my God! Ethan is that baby?" Sophie felt sick to her stomach. "Oh my God! Oh my God! I can't believe it! It…it's…oh my God!" Sophie was close to hyperventilating.

"Sophie!" Winston grew alarmed. "Sophie!"

"What? Oh my God, Winston, it can't be true." Sophie was reflecting back over these last many weeks and felt nauseated.

"It isn't true."

"Pardon?"

"It wasn't Ethan. He is my son with Emily. We had another son…"

"You did?"

"Yes."

"My brother…" she quietly reflected as she slowly calmed down.

"Yes, your brother, and the son of your mother and me."

"Oh." Sophie felt inundated with information. "So, you and my mother had an affair, she got pregnant but she didn't want the baby?"

"She definitely did, however, she said that your father wasn't taking the affair nor the pregnancy well and she was at risk of him leaving her. She didn't feel it was in the best interest of the baby or their relationship and so, soon after she gave birth, your mother rescinded her rights and agreed to let me have full custody of the baby. By that time, I had met Emily and we became engaged to be married."

"That seems rather quick to get over my mother." Sophie was disappointed.

"Emily and I had known each other previously and had become reacquainted, and just knew that we were meant to be together."

Sophie nodded while trying to process everything Winston was telling her.

"So, we discussed it and Emily welcomed the baby into our lives unconditionally."

"Of course, that makes more sense now that it wouldn't have been Ethan. Mother had left a sealed confidential envelope addressed to this lawyer's office regarding Stephen Nolan Callaghan. It was to be delivered here and she said they would know how to contact him."

"Yes, once Emily and I took custody we called him Nolan. Your mother was unaware of that."

"Why the confidential letter?" Sophie was confused.

"Once the letter was opened up, it mentioned that I was his father and of course, one thing led to another and I was contacted. It said inside that your mother didn't want to disclose who I was, to protect myself and Stephen, because she wasn't sure if he knew about her. She was kindly giving me the opportunity to speak to him first had he not known. It explained that she had left something for Stephen in her will and I was to contact her lawyer about it, but I suppose, that would be you at this particular moment. I suppose too, she wouldn't have known whether your father would be alive at the time her will was read, so she would have wanted me to be prepared for any concerns that might arise."

"This is unbelievable." Sophie was at a loss for words.

"I would agree." Winston knew it was a lot of information to take in and sympathized with Sophie.

"But why did you never keep in touch?" Sophie grew momentarily angry.

"Oh, but I did. I discreetly sent your mother pictures, letters, cards from Nolan through my lawyer but they were always returned unopened."

"Why didn't you try harder? Go visit?"

"I was the only one trying so eventually I stopped. Emily and I loved Nolan with all our hearts and when Ethan was born, well…I decided that enough was enough. It wasn't easy, but…"

"But what?"

"But…Emily and I had our own family to consider. The boys didn't know any different. I never did tell Nolan that Emily wasn't his birth mother and Ethan didn't need to know. Years later, I had considered trying again but I heard that she had a daughter…"

"Me."

"Yes, you, so I decided against it. I didn't want to disrupt her life. So much time had passed and I presumed she had moved on for the sake of her relationship with Bernie, your father. I respected that."

"I can't say that I do." Sophie was flabbergasted by her mother's weakness and her father's cold indifference. "How could she not want to see or hear what was happening with her own child?"

"Please don't judge her too harshly, Sophie. It was a complicated time. Her mother disowned her when she heard she was pregnant, while having an affair no less. It was very emotionally difficult for your mother. It was a one-time indiscretion. She was in love with your father and she likely thought it best for all involved to just let things go."

"I find this completely unbelievable. What a tangled web you all wove. Was it really necessary? Why couldn't she have kept the baby? Why couldn't my father have been more accepting and just have dealt with things? Why didn't you tell Nolan, or Ethan, for that matter? It's all so overwhelming and almost unforgivable."

"Please Sophie. It was a different time back then. It was not like today where everything is open and talked about."

"Winston, how could you not tell Ethan about his brother? For that matter, I've been angry at my mother for two years after learning that she had this secret, and now this. My father didn't even know about her will. I can't imagine how he would have felt if he had lived. It's just deception upon deception. You should all be ashamed of yourselves."

"Sophie…" Contemplating what to say, Winston struggled. "Sophie, I've been trying to figure out the best way to tell Ethan. I delayed this meeting as long as possible but…"

"But you need to tell him, Winston. He deserves to know. As does Nolan. Where is Nolan, by the way? Why is he not here with you? Ethan never mentioned a brother."

"Well, sadly, Nolan died several months ago."

"What?" Sophie suddenly felt heartbroken over not meeting the brother she never knew she had to begin with.

"Nolan died of a brain tumour. It was devastating. We loved him very much."

"Oh my God, Winston, that's...I don't know what to say." Sophie was overcome with emotion.

"So, after Nolan died I felt that there really was no point in telling Ethan, to what end? The past was the past." Winston hesitated, "Until now, that is. I was going to speak to Ethan about it all but couldn't bring myself to do so. The right opportunity never seemed to present itself, something always got in the way. So, I decided that perhaps I should speak to, well...to you, first, to see what this is all about and as you know everything had been delayed recently due to my heart attack."

"Oh my God! Yes...I...honestly, I'm so overwhelmed right now. It's not enough that my mother dropped her bombshell on my sister and I, ever so dramatically, through her will but now this."

"I understand that it's a lot."

"To say the least." Sophie was feeling panicky. "I need to think."

Getting up, she walked out of the board room, down the hall and out the front door. She needed air and she needed time to absorb everything Winston just confessed to her.

Sitting in her car, she didn't know what to think, how to feel.

Talking out loud to herself, Sophie was furious. "Oh my God, Mother, you certainly know how to drop a bombshell. Thanks for not telling us everything. How absolutely selfish of you to let Francine and I find out this way. What would daddy have thought if he were still alive? What kind of a fucking coward were you? What the hell were you thinking? How could you give that baby away and want nothing to do with him? How could daddy be so emotionally removed to not want to care for that baby, your baby, regardless of who the father was. You were all friends. You fucked up but that baby…Nolan, deserved to know who his mother was. For Christ sakes what was wrong with all of you?"

Tears were streaming down her cheeks as she yelled.

"Daddy, what the hell? I had a brother and because of you, I never knew him and he died not knowing anything. I'm so angry at you both right now. And how absolutely selfish of Winston to not tell Nolan or Ethan. You should all be ashamed of yourselves. My God, I'm so fucking mad at you all right now! How could you?! Then on top of all of this, because Francine and Tyler fought this for the last two years, we missed out on our opportunity to meet our own brother and he missed out knowing he had more family. Oh my God, I am so fucking angry at everyone!"

Sophie sat thinking about what to do next. It wasn't long before she knew exactly what needed to happen. Wiping the tears away and blowing her nose, Sophie got out of the car, marched back into the office, down the hall and into the board room where Winston sat with Mr. Hawthorne having a coffee and quietly talking.

Looking up, Winston was relieved to see Sophie had returned. He hadn't expected it but had hoped for it.

"Winston, Mr. Hawthorne, right now I'm absolutely livid. I'm angry with my mother and father, and with you too, Winston. I think all three of you should be ashamed of how you handled this entire situation. So, here is what's going to happen. The three of us are going to go over my mother's will and once this is all sorted out then we are going to meet with Ethan. But before that happens, you, Winston, are going to tell him everything."

"He's not going to understand anymore than you did, Sophie..."

"I don't care. He deserves to know. He has the right to know and quite frankly your feelings don't have any bearing on when or how that conversation takes place. Do I make myself perfectly clear?"

Sophie stood staring down Winston. Mr. Hawthorne kept quiet and waited. The room was eerily quiet with the only noise being the distant ringing of phones and the sound of a clock ticking on the wall.

"Winston, it's time to put the past on the table and deal with it."

Winston looked down at his coffee and nodded in agreement.

"Agreed, Sophie. It's long overdue."

Sophie fought back tears. She needed to remain strong. The hard part would be tomorrow, for Winston. She would be there to support Ethan if he was willing.

"Okay then, so let's go over this will and discuss what needs to be done in light of this whole mess that has been uncovered."

Pulling out the paperwork, Sophie asked Mr. Hawthorne if he wanted to read it out loud and he declined allowing Sophie to proceed.

"So, as it turns out my mother never told my father about what was in her will. Why am I not surprised?" Sophie's sarcasm was evident.

"That said, she has left her entire portion of the business to..." Sophie hesitated, "...her son, Stephen...Nolan."

Tears came to Winston's eyes. "Your mother did that?"

"Yes."

"For Nolan?" Winston could hardly speak.

"Yes, for Nolan." Sophie could only imagine how emotional and shocking this moment must be for Winston.

"She'd stated that she knew my sister and I were getting our father's share of the business, knew we would be taken care of. She wanted her son to have her share."

"That must have been upsetting for you and your sister."

"No, the upsetting part for us was not knowing that we had a brother."

Gathering her thoughts, Sophie continued, "My father had stepped down a few years before they died due to health issues, leaving my mother as CEO. Mother named me as her successor and I've been chief executive officer ever since. My father's part of the business, amongst other personal investments, was left to me and my sister, who has no real interest in the business anyway and, who is a silent partner. That said, my sister has been resistant to all of this. Trust me, I've been dealing with her in the courts for the last two years as she tried to prevent this from moving forward."

Winston looked concerned.

"Don't worry, she lost."

Winston nodded.

"Now, in light of this and the fact that my mother's son...Nolan, has recently passed away, then it is stated that his portion would go to his immediate family...children?" Looking at Winston, she asked, "Was Nolan married or did he have any children?"

"No, neither."

"So, what happens now?" Sophie looked at Mr. Hawthorne.

"Well, actually, I think I can resolve this rather easily." Winston spoke up. "Nolan, knowing that he was dying, had a will made up."

Sophie was hopeful that it would be straightforward.

"He actually left everything to his brother, Ethan."

Oh God! Sophie's head was spinning.

This entire situation was truly unbelievable to her. How she met Winston, her relationship with Ethan, and now all of this. It was far more complicated than she had ever anticipated it would be. She was at a loss.

"So, I suppose then, Ethan will inherit Nolan's share of the business." Winston looked over at Mr. Hawthorne who nodded.

Sophie closed her eyes.

What the hell is happening here? I just can't fathom any of this. It's far too much to take in all at once. Hearing about my mother and Winston. Finding out I have a brother, finding out he died and now Ethan is heir to his estate. This is more than any one person should have to deal with.

"Sophie, I know this must be overwhelming." Winston wanted to console her but was unsure how.

Opening her eyes again, Sophie looked at the two men before her.

"You know what? You speak to Ethan and then we will talk. Am I overwhelmed? Absolutely, you bet I am! I'm actually pretty angry as well. At all three of you!"

"Right now, I have a sister who resents the fact that our mother and father lied to us our entire lives, I find out that we have a brother who is entitled to our mother's part of the business. A brother, who, has sadly, died. I've also just found out that my mother had an affair with you, Winston, became pregnant then gave up the baby because of my father's complete selfishness and insecurities and her own cowardice." Sophie took a minute to compose her thoughts.

"Did I expect this to be so damn complicated? Not at all but here I am having to deal with a web of lies; a brother I never had the opportunity to meet; a will that has torn my sister and I apart and one that will most probably be a big problem for you and Ethan. And why? All because you, my father and mother couldn't just plain and simply tell the truth to anyone, including each other. It's repulsive and downright selfish when you consider that the collateral damage is the four individuals who had a right to know all along."

Grabbing her purse and briefcase, Sophie stood up.

"I expect this to be resolved by the end of the day tomorrow."

With that, Sophie left disgusted and angrier than she had been in a very long time.

THIRTY THREE

Arriving back at her suite, Sophie threw herself down on the bed and cried. The entire situation was more than she could deal with at the moment and she needed time to cope with it all.

Crying herself to sleep, Sophie awoke later in the day to her phone ringing. Looking at it, she didn't dare answer it. The last person she wanted to speak to was Ethan. She wouldn't know what to say to him anyway. She knew she had to wait for Winston to speak with him and the eventual fallout from what would most definitely be devastating news for Ethan and very possibly a crippling effect on their relationship.

Walking down to the restaurant for dinner, Sophie ordered and sat quietly sipping on her wine, speculating what would happen once Winston spoke to Ethan. She wondered if he had already spoken to Ethan. Was this going to create a problem between the two men? What would it mean for her and Ethan's relationship?

Looking up, Sophie saw Anika walking across the lobby.

"Anika!"

The other woman turned and smiled when she saw Sophie.

"Do you have a few minutes that I could speak with you about something?"

"Of course. Just give me a moment to drop this package off at the front desk."

Sophie wasn't sure if Anika could help her or not but she knew she needed to get advice from someone she trusted.

"How are you today?" Anika smiled as she sat down and signalled for Marvin to bring her a coffee.

"Well, Anika, I need some advice." Sophie wasn't sure where to begin.

"Absolutely, what can I help you with?"

Marvin placed coffee on the table and left with a nod.

Sophie explained the situation to Anika who maintained her usual calm unassuming demeanour.

"...and so, now I'm not sure what to do about Ethan, or Winston, for that matter. This entire situation is like a bad soap opera. I think Ethan is going to be just as upset as Francine and I were once he discovers the truth. I'm just concerned about how it will affect our relationship. Do I call him, do I wait for him to call me?"

Sitting quietly thinking, Anika sipped on her coffee before speaking.

"Admittedly, I'm sure this is quite a shock as far as your parents are concerned. Of course, it's understandable, especially how you found out."

"It was devastating and now to discover that Nolan has recently passed away. It's so upsetting to think we could have met him, could have had a relationship with him..."

"The past is the past, Sophie. You mustn't torment yourself over it. It cannot be changed. Acceptance will be the only way to move forward from all of this."

"I just don't know if I can move forward from it. My parents lied to us our entire lives. My father was..."

"Human." Anika assured her.

Looking up at Anika, tears came to Sophie's eyes.

"Sophie, you must understand it's different now. There is still a great deal of intolerance but there has been growth and things that we accept or understand better now, that just weren't tolerated back then. It's a different day and age. You must try to understand that."

"It's difficult though."

"Yes, true. The shock of such a confession must be overwhelming but Nolan didn't know any different. He lived with his father. He was loved, had a family who adored him by the sounds of it. And as far as Ethan is concerned, he's a grown man. He will either accept the past or he will allow it to tear his relationship with his father apart. This will show the true character of the man."

"I wouldn't blame him if he was angry about it all, I know I certainly was. This is a bitter pill to swallow, being lied to your entire life. I'm so angry at my parents. I just don't know how to proceed from here with the business, with our family...with Ethan. It's so overwhelming."

"You'll figure it out, Sophie. Go with your heart. Forget your parents and your sister. Forget Winston. They are irrelevant at this junction in time. It's about you and Ethan right now. No one else."

"I suppose." Sophie wasn't entirely convinced.

"You need to decide what you want. Yes, the business complicates things a little..."

"A lot." Sophie shook her head in confusion.

"Okay...a lot. Do you want to see Ethan again on a personal level?"

"Definitely, I have never been so drawn to someone my entire life."

"So, there's decision number one."

Sophie looked at Anika who was beginning to so easily unravel the threads of confusion.

"As far as your mother's estate goes, there is no decision to make. Your mother already made it. What it comes down to is what Ethan will want to do with his brother's inheritance. Will he want to run with it and work with you or will he want to cash out and walk away? These are questions you must wait for the answer on but you are not the one who needs to make those decisions."

"Fair enough." Sophie was grateful that Anika was weeding through the complications of her life and placing them neatly before her.

"What you will need to decide on, is whether you and Ethan want to continue your relationship and can you deal with it if he wants to fully participate in the business. Now that's the complication both you and Ethan need to discuss…together."

"I just don't know how it will work if he decides to become fully involved with the business. We are competitors…"

"How about you take it one step at a time. Wait to see what he decides to do first."

"But the papers need to be signed tomorrow."

"What's the hurry? He may, after all, need some time to absorb the news he is about to receive about his brother. Give him space. Let him come to you when he's ready."

"Thank you, Anika. You've helped to clear some things up for me."

"You'll figure it out."

"I hope so."

"May I add that this could be an opportunity for a business amalgamation should everything work out. Something to think about."

Nodding, Sophie sat quietly thinking.

"Well, I must go. Take a deep breath, Sophie. Mistakes were made in the past but you can perhaps take this time to get to know the brother you never had the opportunity to meet. Try to understand how difficult the entire situation must have been for your parents and Winston. They were imperfect people...like all of us."

Watching Anika leave, Sophie had a lot to think about. Finishing her dinner she headed back to her room.

Ethan hadn't tried to call her for hours and she could only speculate that Winston might have met with him. She was anxious to hear how things went; to know how Ethan was doing; to support him but didn't dare call him.

THIRTY FOUR

By FRIDAY MORNING, SOPHIE AWOKE to her phone ringing. Seeing that it was Mr. Hawthorne she quickly answered.

"Mr. Hawthorne, have you heard from Winston?"

"Unfortunately, there has been a delay..."

"What's the delay? I certainly hope Winston spoke with Ethan. We have a lot to discuss..."

"Ms Callaghan, Winston is in hospital."

"What?! What happened? Where is he?" Sophie immediately grew concerned.

"He's at Granite Hill Memorial Hospital. He has been there since last night."

"But what happened?"

"I was told by his son that their discussion was rather difficult for Winston and he began having chest pains."

"Thank you, Mr. Hawthorne. I'm going to head right over to the hospital to see him."

"I don't know if that is the best idea…"

"I don't care. I'm going."

Arriving at the emergency department, Sophie rushed to the triage desk.

"Can I help you?" The nurse showed a genuine lack of interest.

"I'm looking for Winston Blackburn. I understand he was brought in here last night?

"Are you family?"

Sophie hesitated. *Not this again.*

"Are you family?" The nurse grew impatient.

"Yes, she's family." A familiar voice echoed across the room.

Looking back, tears came to Sophie's eyes.

"Ethan. How's your dad?"

"He will be fine."

Walking towards each other, Ethan said, "It seems that, once again, we have a lot to talk about."

Sophie nodded then began to cry. "I'm so confused."

Ethan pulled her into his arms and hugged her. "Me too but it's going to be alright."

"I'm so sorry, Ethan."

"You have nothing to be sorry about. This wasn't your doing. Let's face it, we've both been blindsided by all of this."

Pulling away, Ethan looked deeply into Sophie's eyes, hands gently holding her by the shoulders.

"We have lots of time to talk. The doctor is with dad right now so let's go for a walk."

Nodding, Sophie walked with Ethan outside and across the road to a park. This was not how she wanted to see Ethan again and certainly not when or where she wanted to discuss her mother's estate with him.

Walking through the park, dry leaves crunched under their feet as they walked. Sophie wasn't sure where to begin.

"What's going on with your dad?"

"He will be fine. He had a panic-attack."

"Understandable."

"Agreed. He was pretty stressed out when he spoke with me about Nolan."

"I can't help but take some of the blame for that." Sophie recalled her conversation the day before at Mr. Hawthorne's office.

"He said you were pretty tough on him."

"Wouldn't you have been?"

"I was, actually."

"Weren't you angry to find out you had been lied to your whole life?"

"Definitely...at first, but hearing the entire story, I softened."

"You're far more understanding than I am." Sophie wasn't sure whether to be angry with herself or justified in her resentment.

"Listen, take it easy on your mom and dad. They were young. Think about it. They were in their twenties. They were scared, judged by everyone around them. Your mother was disowned by her own mother. What would you have done?"

"I can tell you I certainly wouldn't have given up my baby."

"But your mother really didn't 'give him up'."

"She most certainly did!"

"She let his father raise him and there is nothing wrong with that. Put yourself in her shoes, Sophie. Your mother did the right thing for him. She put her feelings aside and did what was best for her baby. I give her full credit for her lack of selfishness. It's the past and yes, you, your sister and me were all given some shocking news but in the end Nolan was in a loving home with his father."

"But my father was such a jerk about it all. I get that he was hurt but…"

"But he loved your mother enough to forgive her and move on and I think we need to do the same. Love all three of them enough to move on from this."

"I'm just really heartbroken that I didn't have a chance to meet Nolan."

"He would have loved you and you him." Ethan smiled. "The two of you would have been nothing but trouble together, I've no doubt."

Nodding, Sophie began to cry.

"Sophie, in the end, there is a lot of good coming out of all of this. We now know the truth. I can assure you that my mother loved Nolan like her own. She knew all along who Nolan was and it didn't matter to her, in her eyes he was her son. Your mother allowed another woman to help raise her son, so there was a lot of love happening here. They thought they were doing what was best for all involved. I think we need to accept this. They certainly could."

"I suppose so. It's just been such an emotional roller-coaster these last two years and now all of this." Thinking for a moment she asked, "How is your dad taking everything? I feel terrible that he had a panic-attack."

"Yes, well, he's fine and will be fine. He was more concerned about how I would take the news. To be honest, after the initial shock, I thought it was a rather interesting love story that has now drawn our two families together in more ways than one. You have to admit, there is nothing more interesting than some family history drama."

Ethan was trying to make light of things hoping that Sophie could forgive her parents.

"I can see your point. God knows my family history has definitely reached a whole new level of interesting." Sophie was able to laugh.

"There, you see? Life would be rather boring if everything went like clockwork."

"Admittedly, I panicked when I thought the son was you. Now that would have been extremely awkward."

"Actually, Dad still doesn't know about us."

"Really? When exactly were you planning on telling him?"

"I don't think I need to explain to you that the one opportunity I had was when he dropped this bombshell on me. Didn't seem like the right time to elaborate."

"Isn't it funny how history repeats itself? My mother and your father and now you and I."

"So what are we going to do about this inheritance? I kind of like the idea of working side by side with you." Ethan grinned.

Peeking into the exam room, Sophie smiled to see Winston sitting up and appearing to be no worse for the wear.

"Sophie, my dear, please come in."

Ethan quietly followed behind her.

"Winston, I'm so sorry. I should have been more understanding of what must have been a very difficult time for you, for all of you."

"It's fine, I'm fine. It was a very long time ago and as much as I loved your mother at the time, Sophie, I fell in love and married an extraordinary woman in Emily. A woman who welcomed my child into our home as her own with such love. Nolan had a wonderful life and although he died far too young, he never once doubted how we felt about him."

"I would have liked to have met him and for that I'm angry at my parents and my sister for that matter. I will get over it but I hope to learn more about him, get to know him through stories and pictures from you and Ethan."

"Indeed you will."

There was a moment of awkward silence before Winston asked, "What are we going to do about this inheritance?"

"Well, Dad, Sophie and I have had a discussion about that."

"You have. Already?"

"Yes, and we have agreed to work together. What that looks like at the moment we haven't figured out but we will. It will be a work in progress for now, however, it's one that we are both looking forward to."

Winston looked over to Sophie.

"This is good news?"

"Yes, very good news." Sophie smiled then looked over to Ethan.

"Dad…"

"Yes?"

Just then the doctor walked in with his chart.

"Okay, Mr. Blackburn, we are going to release you on the condition that you learn to relax. Your body can't take all the stress that you have been under so soon after your heart attack. No work, no stress…relaxation only. Can you manage to do that?" Dr. Ritchler looked over the top of his glasses at Winston.

"He can." Ethan gave a stern look in his father's direction. "He will."

Thinking briefly, Winston said, "I can, doctor. I plan on retiring from the family business, anyway. My son will be taking over."

Ethan was shocked to hear this unexpected announcement.

"Dad?"

Sophie just stood silent. She knew life was going to be very different from here on for all of them. Hearing her phone ring, she saw that it was Tony calling.

Answering it, she quietly said, "Not now, Tony."

"But..."

"I said, not now."

"But your sister is constantly calling. What am I supposed to tell her?" Tony maintained his control but Sophie could tell he was growing frustrated with Francine.

"Tell her, it's done. The papers are signed and we have a new business partner." Hanging up the phone, Sophie was anxious to hear the remainder of the conversation.

"You heard me. I'm retiring. It's time you took over and ran things, Ethan. I've had enough." Winston smiled with satisfaction.

"Excellent! Well then, I don't expect to see you back here." The doctor wrote some notes on the chart and left the room.

THIRTY FIVE

The next day, Sophie was on the phone trying to reason with Tony.

"Tony, I know Francine is upset but it's done."

"*You* say that, *I* realize that, but I can assure you Francine is *not* accepting that." Tony sounded exasperated.

"Well, I'll be back in a few days and will meet with her and Tyler and get them off your back." Sophie reassured him.

"Thank you and I'll look forward to my raise and coffee…"

"Understood." Sophie chuckled.

"By the way…I hate to even ask with all the craziness you're dealing with but could I ask a favour?"

Explaining his favour, Sophie wasn't at all surprised by it.

"I will have the perfect opportunity today."

"Thanks so much, Sophie. This means a lot."

"I know it does, Tony, and it's no trouble. Now go home. It's Saturday. Enjoy the weekend with that handsome man of yours."

Hanging up the phone, Sophie walked out onto the balcony and leaned against the railing, looking out over the city. The sun was shining and reflecting back onto the building windows. The noise of the city was almost calming. The horns blaring, sirens wailing and whistles of traffic cops blowing never seemed to change. She really loved it here in Granite Hill. She was going to miss it when she left. There was a slight breeze that gently swept through her hair. Closing her eyes, she smiled.

Mom, Dad, I'm working on forgiving you but you have to understand, you were always larger than life to me. It's hard to realize that you were only human, that you were once young people living in a time that was far less forgiving than the world we live in now. All I can do is try to understand how difficult your life must have been back then through all of that. Decisions needed to be made and you made them to the best of your ability. I can't begin to comprehend how torn you must have been.

Looking out over the city once again, Sophie felt peace for the first time in over two years. There were still things to sort out but there was still closure for her, closure for her mother and yes, closure for the Blackburn men.

That afternoon, Sophie met with Ethan in the lobby of the hotel. Looking across to the check-in desk, Sophie waved to Anika who smiled warmly seeing the two together.

Getting into Ethan's car, Sophie was curious. "Ethan, where are we going?" Sophie never did think to ask when he called to say he was coming over.

"Some place I think you need to see." Ethan smiled.

They drove about half an hour before pulling into a large gated estate. Driving along a road lined with mature trees, Sophie thought how beautiful it was. Turning a corner, they came to a clearing and tears came to her eyes. She knew now where they were going.

Getting out of the car, Ethan indicated for her to follow him. Walking a short distance, they stopped, and Ethan smiled.

"I thought this was a good place to start for you to get to know your brother."

Reading the monument, Sophie began to cry.

Stephen Nolan Blackburn

A shining light to all who knew him.

September 17, 1970 – July 23, 2020

Feeling Ethan place his arms around her, the floodgates opened and Sophie turned and sobbed on his shoulder. She could no longer suppress the emotions of the last couple of years. It had all been so much and these last few days had been immensely emotional.

After a few moments, Sophie regained her composure. They stood quietly looking at Nolan's monument.

"Ethan, was Nolan like you?" She was curious to learn more about him.

"Nothing like me, thank God!"

They both laughed.

"Seriously though, he had a big heart and was a passionate person, much like you."

"Did he not have a girlfriend...wife?"

"Unfortunately, no. He was what you would call the stereotypical bachelor. He just wasn't the type who wanted to settle down. When he was in university he had been in love with a girl but her parents forbade her to marry him. Different religions, different beliefs. She was younger than Nolan. Her parents forced her to return home and into an arranged marriage. Nolan was devastated and just couldn't find it in himself to get beyond his love for her."

"That's so heartbreaking."

"After he graduated, Nolan threw himself into his work. He scouted cities around the world for potential new hotel builds. He loved the travel and could envision hotels in some of the most obscure places, but they almost always seemed to work out. Dad was confident in him. If Nolan said we should build or develop a new hotel in a specific location, then dad went with it knowing that Nolan had an eye for the future."

"That's incredible."

"In fact, it was Nolan who came across Omolara Orphanage during his travels and came home insistent we needed to help. This is one of the reasons that I have been so passionate about helping this cause, especially after his death. "

"I see." Sophie grew reflective. "He sounds remarkable."

"He was. Words can't express how much I miss him. We used to spend a lot of time together growing up, playing tennis, going to baseball games, we were always together. He was my best friend."

Nodding, Sophie craved more information but also knew she wasn't ready for it all just yet.

"Thank you, Ethan. This means so much to me."

"You're welcome." Ethan gave her a few minutes then asked, "Are you free for dinner tonight? Dad wants us to come over if you are up for it."

"I'm not sure I should go until you've spoken to him about us."

"Oh, he knows. I told him last night."

"You did! How did he react?" Sophie was apprehensive.

"To say he was thrilled is an understatement. He thinks the world of you, Sophie, and not just because you saved his life." Ethan grinned.

"Hmmm, yes, I suppose that in itself would be a good reason to like someone." She laughed. "Okay, sure, dinner it is."

After Ethan dropped her off at the hotel, Sophie headed up to her room and ordered up a bottle of wine.

Sitting out on the balcony, she decided this was as good a time as any to celebrate and take some time out to absorb all that had taken place in the last few days and just unwind. She admittedly had mixed emotions, on one hand she was very happy that she managed to execute her mother's will but on the other hand, sad to not have had the opportunity to meet Nolan...her brother. It was really a very bittersweet moment. She loved her parents, even though she was still angry about some things. It would take time to completely heal from the hurt, but she was trying to understand what it must have been like for them back then. She wondered if her mother ever wondered about Nolan, who he was as a person, what he looked like.

Before she knew it, Sophie had finished off the bottle of wine, a package of potato chips and was headed to the bar fridge for more.

A few hours later, she heard a knock on the door. It took her several moments to acknowledge what the noise was. Standing up, she stumbled over her shoes. Trying to get her footing again, she attempted to stop her head from spinning but no matter how hard she held her head with her hands, it wouldn't stop.

Again, she heard a door knock.

Gaining her footing, she attempted to walk once again in the direction of the noise. This time she watched her feet very carefully as she took each step. They didn't seem to be working very well. Stumbling over to the couch, she fell face first over the back of it and struggled to push herself back up again.

More knocking.

"Sophie, are you there?"

"Quit yelling! I'm coming, I'm coming."

Finally, arriving at the door, Sophie had a hard time focusing on the door handle but finally managed to get the door open using both of her hands together.

"Well, hello…what's your name again?"

"Sophie?"

"Your name's Sophie, too?" Her eyes opened wide with surprise.

"Are you drunk?" Ethan was astonished to see her swaying as she looked at him with unfocussed eyes.

"Yup."

And with that, she fell down and passed out.

THIRTY SIX

WAKING UP, SOPHIE STRUGGLED TO focus in the darkness. Glancing over at the bedside clock, it took her a couple of minutes to actually see the time, and that only happened when she narrowed her eyes. She was shocked to see that it was just after midnight.

Finally, pulling herself to a sitting position, she looked down and noticed a garbage can sitting next to the bed.

"That can't be a good sign and who put it there?"

Walking out to the sitting room, Sophie smiled seeing Ethan asleep on the couch with the television going.

Grabbing a blanket off the bed, she covered him up, turned off the television then crawled back into bed and promptly fell asleep.

⤳⤳

"Wakey wakey. Rise and shine."

Ethan's voice was far too perky for her this particular morning.

"Oh my God, my head hurts. Please whisper."

"I think someone might have a hangover this morning." Ethan teased.

"Oh shut the hell up." Sophie muttered in response.

"Here, I think you could use this water. Drink up."

Lying on the bed, she realized she was still fully dressed. Sitting up, she drank the water.

"What the hell? I only had some wine. How could I be this hungover?"

"Ah, but that isn't all you had."

"It's not?"

"Noooo, not by a long shot. Pardon the pun." He laughed rather unsympathetically.

"You, in fact, had a bottle of wine, two beer, and to top it all off several of those little tiny bottles of liquor from the bar fridge."

"Seriously?"

"Six to be exact."

"Really? How the hell did I manage to drink all of that?"

"Oh, and might I add, all on pretty much of an empty stomach, although, it seems you did manage to eat a small package of potato chips."

"I see."

"Oh, and if you recall, we were supposed to have dinner with my father last night." Ethan wasn't angry, in fact, he was more amused thinking about how badly Sophie was likely feeling after her solo drunken soiree.

"That is so not good." Sophie groaned.

Hearing a knock, Ethan opened the door, tipped the server and pushed the food cart into the living room.

"I ordered us in some breakfast so I hope you're hungry."

The smell of food turned Sophie's stomach. Running to the washroom she immediately threw up.

I suspect that was long overdue.

Washing her face and brushing her teeth, she felt much better. Walking out of the washroom, the smell of the food still wasn't appealing but at least she didn't feel sick anymore.

"Guess I'm eating alone." Ethan tried not to laugh.

"Yeah, you're eating alone."

Pouring herself a coffee, she walked out to the balcony and sat down. Taking in a deep breath of fresh air, she shut her eyes from the bright morning sun.

Ethan followed closely behind with a plate full of food.

"So, I guess you needed a good night of drinking?"

"That I did."

"Everything okay?"

"Yeah, everything's okay."

Sipping on her coffee, Sophie knew it was going to take time to feel herself again after her night of drinking.

Sitting quietly, a few minutes later Ethan asked, "Need some Tylenol?"

"Yup. And some Gravol."

THIRTY SEVEN

Having slept the afternoon away, Sophie awoke feeling refreshed and headache free. Walking out to the living room, she found a note from Ethan that he would be picking her up by seven o'clock to meet with Winston for dinner.

Sophie felt ready to meet the evening and was unsurprisingly starving.

By seven o'clock there was a knock at the door. Opening it up, she was greeted by Ethan.

"Ah, I see you are looking much more yourself this evening." He laughed.

"Yes, I'm feeling much better."

Heading downstairs, they were hopping into his car when Sophie remembered she had something to ask him and figured now was as good a time as any.

"Ethan, I have a favour to ask of you, for a friend."

"Okay, sure. What is it?"

Sophie explained the situation to Ethan who was more than happy to help out. Sophie was ecstatic as they went over the details.

"We can deal with all of that tomorrow morning. I'll set up an appointment."

"Thanks so much, Ethan. This is so exciting."

Arriving at Winston's, Sophie and Ethan were once again greeted by Paige who was sure to point out that Winston was to remain calm and not to discuss any business, whatsoever.

"Do I make myself perfectly clear?" Paige was firm and stared Ethan and Sophie down waiting for confirmation that they would abide by her rules before allowing them entry.

"Very." They both quickly confirmed.

After dinner and much conversation about their recent connections, Winston said, "I suspected when I saw your necklace that you could possibly have been related to Kathleen but thought it was too coincidental to be a reality."

"Why do you say that?" Sophie was confused.

"Full disclosure?"

"Yes, please do. My God, there have been so many bombshells dropped lately that I couldn't be any more surprised than I already have been, although I have said that before."

"I actually had given that necklace to your mother from Nolan after he came to live with me."

"You did? But she said her mother gave it to her."

"Ah yes, well, I suspect that was to avoid telling your father the truth."

"Why am I not surprised she had a cover story? More secrets." Sophie looked down at the necklace around her neck. "You know…she wore it every day."

Smiling, Winston looked up at Sophie, "Nolan's initials are engraved inside the heart. Here, let me show you."

Removing the necklace, Sophie handed it to Winston who pointed them out to her.

Tears came to her eyes.

"I'm sorry…I've upset you."

"No Winston, it actually means so much more to me now, than it did before. Thank you for telling me."

"Okay you two. Sophie and I must bid you adieu or we will have Paige chasing us out." Ethan walked over and gave his father a hug. "I'll let Paige know we are leaving. I'll be home later on."

"Behave yourself, Winston. No more hospital visits." Sophie gave him a hug and then a kiss on the cheek.

"Good-bye you two. I must admit, I'm very happy for the two of you. It gives closure to everything, in my humble opinion."

Reaching the library doors, Sophie stopped and turned around.

"I'm curious, Winston, what was the name of that hotel you and my parents started up together?"

"The Stargazing Hotel."

THIRTY EIGHT

THE NEXT DAY, AFTER HEARING back from Ethan, Sophie called Tony.

"You and Jeff need to get on the next train...plane...car...whatever, and get here by tomorrow afternoon."

"What?! Are you kidding me? Tell me you're serious."

"I'm dead serious. Use the company credit card, I'll approve it myself. Just tell anyone asking that I've requested you come here to assist me with business matters."

"Oh my God, Sophie, thank you so much."

"I'll see you both tomorrow. I'll pick you up...just let me know when and where."

By three o'clock the next day, Sophie was sitting at the train station waiting for Tony and Jeff to arrive. Hearing the train whistle in the distance, Sophie grew very excited.

As the train hissed into the station, the whistle was deafening as it announced their arrival.

It took time but Sophie soon saw Tony and Jeff walk down the steps, and ran up to greet them.

"Okay you two, we have a meeting to go to, right now."

"Sophie we can't thank you enough, truly, this means so much to us." Jeff became emotional.

"No worries, Jeff. Let's get this done. There are no two people more deserving of this help."

Jeff was taller than Tony and just as handsome. He was blond with blue eyes whereas Tony had dark hair and brown eyes. Both were very fashionable dressers. Sophie often teased Tony about his expensive taste in clothes, but she had to admit that he always looked impeccable.

Pulling up in front of the office, Sophie got out of the car. The two men got out and stood staring at the sign.

"Omolara Orphanage and Adoption Agency. Oh my God, I'm so nervous." Tony put his arm around Jeff to comfort him.

"Well, there's no time to waste, so let's go." Sophie ushered them along into the building where they met a waiting Ethan.

"Tony, Jeff, this is Ethan Blackburn. He is co-chair of the board of directors here, and is the person you have to thank for arranging all of this."

"Not true. Sophie advocated on your behalf. I'm just the person to point you in the right direction."

"Thank you so much, Ethan."

"It's a pleasure to meet you both. Now, this is what's going to happen."

Ethan explained the process to both men who were extremely nervous but knew this was the pathway to their dream. They wanted to be parents and their dream was finally about to be realized.

Following Ethan onto an elevator and up to the fourth floor, they all walked down a long hallway to a meeting room. Through the door, they were greeted by a young woman with a big smile on her face.

"Hello, my name is Sylvia St. Ives and I'm Executive Director here at Omolara. Please take a seat.

"We will leave and give you all some privacy. Take your time."

Sophie hugged Tony and whispered in his ear. "You've got this, just be yourself."

EPILOGUE

EIGHTEEN MONTHS LATER

"I'M SO NERVOUS."

"Just take a deep breath, Sophie. This is your dream come true. Now, let me have a good look at you." Tony fussed with her hair for a minute, ensuring every strand was in place.

"Is Ethan here?" Sophie adjusted her dress.

"Yes, Ethan is here."

"And what about the minister?"

"Yes, the minister is here, too. Sophie, you're worrying about things you don't need to worry about."

"Jeff! What about Jeff and little Josh. Are they here?"

"Yes, of course they are here. They just arrived."

"I can't believe Josh is three already. Where does the time go?" Thinking for a moment she asked, "Jeff has the rings, right?"

"Yes, he does. Sophie...relax. Everything is going like clockwork."

"I just wish Francine could have made it."

"I know it's disappointing but there was nothing that could be done."

"I think she still resents me for everything…"

Sophie knew that Francine and Tyler had been furious to learn that the estate had been settled once and for all and that Ethan was going to take over Nolan's part of the business. There had been nothing Sophie could say or do to ease the hurt and anger Francine had felt when she found out the two chains were amalgamating. It compounded an already deep resentment. It wasn't long after the amalgamation announcement, that Francine and Tyler relocated to New York City, allowing Francine to finally pursue her dream of acting.

"But, she did agree to come, and she did try to get here. The weather just didn't cooperate." Tony tried to console her.

"It just would have been nice to have my sister here, since my parents aren't." Sophie became teary-eyed.

"Now, don't you dare cry, it will ruin your make-up."

"Maybe we should have postponed this. A last minute wedding…what was I thinking? It's been a busy time, what with amalgamating the businesses, Ethan's move here to Cedardale, not to mention, Francine and Tyler moving to New York City. It's been a lot of change. What if this is a big mistake, Tony. Perhaps we should have just waited until next year to give us more time, actually invite some guests, have my sister here…"

"Sweetheart…and, let me be very clear, I know I work for you, but you will understand when I say…give your damn head a shake! It's the perfect time. An intimate ceremony with the man you love, who loves you, with people who care about you, all right here. There is no doubt, it's the ideal time. Now, get your brave on and go get married."

Hearing the music, Tony smiled at Sophie. "It's time."

"Oh my God!" Sophie closed her eyes.

"You look stunning in your mother's wedding dress."

"Thank you, Tony." Fiddling with her necklace, Sophie was happy to wear it and bring along a little piece of Nolan with her. "And thank you for agreeing to be best man."

"I am honoured, but I must go and get that man of yours to the altar."

Tony walked out leaving Sophie alone with her thoughts. Smelling her bouquet settled her nerves just a little.

"Mom, Dad, I love you both so much. I need to say one thing. Mom, as much as I was angry with you for making me executor of your will, for the bombshell you dropped on us and all the lies and deception over the years, well...I just want to say, thank you. I have met and am about to marry the man I love because of you. I guess that tangled web you all wove worked out in the most unexpected way."

Taking a deep breath in and then out, she walked out to the foyer. Sophie smiled when she saw Winston, looking ever so handsome in his tuxedo, patiently waiting for his future daughter-in-law. As she approached, he held his arm out for her and smiled.

"You look absolutely stunning, my dear. You rival your mother's beauty."

"Thank you, Winston."

"Thank you for allowing me to walk you down the aisle. I'm humbled to step in for a very remarkable man who would have been very proud of you right now."

Sophie fought back tears and reached out for Winston's arm. Turning to look into the near empty chapel, Sophie looked left to see Anika looking radiant holding a bouquet of mixed flowers.

Just then, Jeff quietly snuck past holding Josh's hand. Watching as he handed Josh the small satin pillow with the rings on it, she smiled as Jeff sent him down the aisle before her. He looked absolutely adorable in his little tuxedo, bow tie and curly black hair. He was the perfect ring bearer for their wedding.

Even though Sophie knew there was no turning back now, she did become momentarily apprehensive.

Maybe I should wait. What's to stop me? I mean after all, it's not too late. What if I'm making a big mistake? Maybe I shouldn't be doing this. It seems so quick...

Looking up, Sophie's thoughts were interrupted as she watched a very handsome and dignified Ethan in his tuxedo walk up to the altar, reach out to shake the minister's hand and in doing so, tripped over the step, sending him onto his hands and knees. She shook her head and smiled, watching Tony help him up as they laughed together over Ethan's very undignified misstep.

Right then...in that very moment...right then...Sophie knew she had to marry that man.

"Okay, let's do this!"

OTHER BOOKS BY
L.A. DONAHOE

Just Their Luck

Her Flawsome Life

JUST THEIR LUCK

Moving on from a broken relationship, Sarah's struggles begin from the moment she arrives in Forestville after having a run-in with handsome firefighter Sam Ward. Finding him rude and completely unreasonable, Sarah regrets ever meeting him; a feeling that is clearly mutual.

Having recently ended a tempestuous relationship, Sam has no patience for irrational and short-tempered Sarah Roberts, yet with every encounter Sam finds himself increasingly attracted to her.

Amidst her struggles dealing with Sam, further problems arise for Sarah when her ex-boyfriend Travis Boynton, star quarterback for the Watertown Broncos, decides he has revenge to seek following the end of their turbulent relationship, leaving Sarah wondering how to deal with Travis' escalating scare tactics and her growing feelings towards Sam.

"A thoroughly entertaining read complete with interesting characters, humour, romance and suspense. This book is everything you could want in an easy-to-read page-turner."

L.A. Donahoe has developed a plot and characters that keep the reader interested and involved. The storyline is humorous at times, depicting people and their activities in a small town life. It's an easy read.

"Thank you for your book 'Just Their Luck'. I just finished it and I thoroughly enjoyed it...You had a great combination of romance, fun and drama which made it hard to put down. Loved the characters and who couldn't love George and Karen! I really like your writing style and can't wait for your next book! Happy writing!"

"This could totally be a Hallmark movie!"

HER FLAWSOME LIFE

Life for Quinn Fairchild just isn't going according to plan.

Her ex-fiancé is a cad, her boss a degenerate, her love life not exactly impassioned, interaction with her parents just plain exhausting, and meeting handsome stranger, Darcy, is just another emotional complication she has no desire to get caught up in. She finds him far too presumptuous and confident for her liking and yet, admittedly, there is an undeniable attraction…too much so for her own comfort.

Insistent, that going on a date with Darcy is not a good idea, her best friend, Francois, disagrees. After giving in to her friend's pestering, it isn't long before Quinn regrets that decision, validating that her night out with Darcy was a big mistake and the worst date ever! So, why would she ever consider a second?

"What better way to spend a rainy day than curled up with a good book. I thoroughly enjoyed 'Her Flawsome Life'. It has a strong female character, romance, lust and humour. It is deep enough to keep you turning the pages but light enough to take your mind off of the things happening in the world right now. Can't wait for the next book to come out."

"I just finished my marathon reading of 'Her Flawsome Life'. I couldn't put it down and enjoyed every minute! Looking forward to your next book!"

"Her Flawsome Life was a true joy to read. The characters are so vivid that I wondered if they were based on real people. Francois was definitely a favourite character whom I would love to have as a best friend. Witty, fun, relaxing, and a real page turner. I looked forward to returning home every evening so that I could find out what would happen next. Well done, L.A. Donahoe! I look forward to your next book."

www.ingramcontent.com/pod-product-compliance
Lightning Source LLC
Chambersburg PA
CBHW071138260626
47162CB00003B/831

* 9 7 8 0 2 2 8 5 0 4 0 9 2 *